# Legends of Cthulhu & Other Nightmares

# Legends of Cthulhu & Other Nightmares

Sam Stone

First Published in 2019 by Telos Publishing Ltd,
139 Whitstable Road, Canterbury, Kent CT2 8EQ, UK.

www.telos.co.uk

Telos Publishing Ltd values feedback. Please e-mail us with any comments you may have about this book to:
feedback@telos.co.uk

ISBN: 978-1-84583-134-9



British Library Cataloguing in Publication Data. A catalogue record for this book is available from the British Library.

# Contents

# Legends of Cthulhu

# The Bastet Society

'You never know if you like something unless you try it,' Skye said.

She held out a fork of mushy looking haggis but Kurtis shook his head.

'It's not for me thanks.'

'Vegetarian then?' she asked, viewing his plateful of pasta and vegetables.

'Nope. But I don't eat the innards of things. And that,' he pointed at Skye's plate, which was full of neaps and tatties, as well as the offensive haggis, 'is innards.'

The bell rang, Kurtis grabbed his plate and, without even saying goodbye, moved on. He almost stumbled in his haste to get away.

They were 'Speed Dating with Food' – it was a new fad. You were judged by the food you ate as well as the conversation. Skye had known that she was not Kurtis's type, and it wasn't the food she was eating that turned him away.

She just had no luck whatsoever with men. Despite the fact that she was attractive, something about her always put them off. She didn't know why. Maybe it was her over-pale skin. Perhaps they realized that the caramel highlights in her white hair was not a quirk, but was the only colour that would retain in her albino hair. They saw the taint she carried in her blood line, no matter how she tried to hide it. She was fortunate that her eyes were blue and not pink, or that would have made her lack of pigment more obvious.

Skye put her fork back on the plate as the next man sat down at her table. As she looked up, all thoughts of the black, sleek Kurtis, went completely from her mind.

'I'm Tadeo,' the man said. His voice was smooth with the hint of an accent that Skye couldn't place. 'I was born in Egypt.'

Skye found herself smiling back at Tadeo's perfect white toothed grin. He was certainly striking – with warm golden skin, which looked as though it had been freshly touched by the sun.

'I think you and I are going to get along,' Tadeo said and he dipped his fork into Skye's haggis, scooping up a mouthful, which he ate with obvious enjoyment.

She responded by trying his food. It was black pudding, one of her favourite breakfast dishes.

'I think I've found what I was looking for,' Tadeo said.

They left without finishing their food or before Skye said a word.

Three weeks of sex, booze and carnivorous food blurred into heady obsession. Tadeo was in Skye's thrall.

'I want you to meet some of my friends,' he told her as he fell back against the sheets, soaked with sweat from their exertions. 'I think they'll like you.'

Up until then, their relationship was based on sensation: food and sex. Friends, family and day jobs hadn't come into it. Skye assumed Tadeo had a job, but liked the mystery of not knowing what. Equally she never discussed her dull day life.

Now, Tadeo's suggestion that she meet his friends threw Skye into a state of confusion tinged with panic. What did Tadeo think their relationship was about? Skye herself saw it as a sexual fling that probably wouldn't last, but Tadeo's invitation changed things.

She had never said 'no' to anything he had suggested and this was such a minor thing – compared to his usually inventive depravity which included biting her neck at the same time as vigorously fucking her from behind – that she saw no need to refuse. Even so, as she agreed to go, she couldn't help shuddering with an odd excitement as she replayed his words about his friends: *I think they'll like you …*

Skye knew Tadeo was too good to be true. She had been let down so many times that she couldn't help being cynical about relationships. Often her lack of trust was instrumental in the ending of them. That was when the man stayed around long enough after their first casual fuck. The Tadeo *obsession* wasn't burning out, and this would normally be the moment for Skye to back away, excusing herself from becoming part of his life on a more permanent basis. Like a rabbit caught in headlights, Skye would run for the trees, escaping commitment in the nick of time. This time, however, she didn't feel the urge to flee.

Before he left, sometime after midnight, Tadeo left a card at the side of the bed. 'The address.'

After he left, Skye picked up the card. No name. Just an address.

The house was in Hammersmith, an expensive part of London. Tadeo arranged to meet her there at eight in the evening. Skye caught the Hammersmith and City line to Hammersmith station, then took a short taxi ride and found herself on the front steps of a palatial old house.

*This place must be worth a fortune,* she thought. She looked at the card again, checked the address which was printed in a handwriting-style font. Italicized. *Fancy.* She should have realized that Tadeo's secret life would be extravagant. He didn't have the tastes of a man who worried about money.

At the top of the steps, Skye noticed there was a bronze plaque on the wall beside the door. It read THE BASTET SOCIETY.

*So this is some form of club then ...*

The door opened and Skye looked up at a tall man who was wearing a formal dinner suit. Skye was in jeans – even though they were designer – and a white crop top: she was clearly underdressed. She experienced a momentary feeling of annoyance that Tadeo hadn't advised her of a dress code.

'You must be Skye,' the man said in a clipped English accent. 'Tadeo has told me a lot about you.'

'Really? He's told me *nothing* about you ...' Skye bit her lip. Sometimes she had no filter.

'I'm Sebastian. Do come in.'

Skye followed Sebastian into a large hallway. 'I thought there was a party here tonight?' she said.

'There is a ... gathering,' Sebastian said.

They walked through the silent hallway. Skye had expected to hear music, laughter, the sound of other people in the house. She began to feel peculiar about being there, especially if she was alone with Sebastian. Had Tadeo somehow set her up? After all she really didn't know him at all, did she?

'This way ...'

A nervous anxiety pricked at Skye's skull as she followed Sebastian past a wide staircase towards a door at the end of the long corridor.

*Wait. I didn't ring the bell,* she thought.

'Where *is* Tadeo?' she asked.

'Downstairs.'

Sebastian opened the door to a grand parlour. The room was furnished with plush sofas and chairs positioned before an ornate fireplace.

'Wait here.' He pointed to a small round table where a glass of red wine was poured. 'For you.'

Skye took the seat next to the table but ignored the wine. She wasn't comfortable in this ostentatious house, or club, or whatever it was. She had the suspicion that all was not as it appeared to be, and that wisdom brought about a physical, rather than mental, urge to run.

To distract herself she looked around the room. The walls were full of old paintings of men and women in old fashioned clothing. One she recognized as Elizabethan style because of the rigid collar that the men and women wore in that period. One particular picture looked a lot like Queen Elizabeth I: a red haired woman wearing a dress with broad puffed out sleeves and a stiff round collar circling her throat. This woman wasn't the former queen, however. She was far more attractive, and somewhat feline - perhaps even decadent - in her posture. The woman intrigued her and she studied this picture for quite a while before becoming bored.

The other pictures made her nervous. Even as she stood and moved around the room, those ancient eyes bore into her. Watching her. Judging her from their dust-filled graves ...

Skye tried to shake away those morbid thoughts. It wasn't like her to *think* – she wasn't normally so inventive. She tried to laugh at the cliché she was building in her mind: her senses still screamed at her to leave. All humour fled from her mind.

Now and again she glanced at the door, expecting Sebastian to return with Tadeo, but the house remained silent. Skye's nerves became fragmented. She was twitchy. And the paintings became a source of intimidation. Fifty pairs of dead eyes sucked at her soul. They weighed her down until she sank back into the chair and just stared at the door, willing it to open.

More than half an hour passed before Skye decided enough was enough. Perhaps this was one of Tadeo's games. She was being tested in some way, and suddenly she didn't like it, didn't want to play.

She picked up her purse and walked towards the door determined to leave even though that would probably mean the end of her relationship with Tadeo. Perhaps that was for the best anyway. It had gone on much longer than it should have.

The door opened as she reached for the handle.

'There you are!' said Tadeo. 'I did say eight. It's now eight thirty-five.'

'I've been here for over half an hour,' Skye said.

'Oh?'

'You're friend Sebastian let me in.'

'You *saw* Sebastian?'

'Yes. He told me to wait in here.'

'Next you'll be telling me these painting are all of people,' Tadeo laughed.

'What do you mean? They are ...'

As Skye turned around she saw that the paintings had changed. Where the Elizabethan woman had been, a pretty ginger cat lay across a plush chair. Her eyes flicked over the other paintings. All of them were of cats – not people.

'Is this some kind of joke?' Skye said. Somehow, they had been switched when her back was turned ...

'Come and meet the gang,' said Tadeo

'Gang?'

'My friends. They are waiting to meet you in the entertaining room.'

Skye followed Tadeo from the parlour, glancing back at the paintings again as she left the room. She would question him later on his joke. Now was not the time.

In the corridor she could hear music and laughter and the blur of conversations behind dense walls. Tadeo opened up a double set of doors and walked into a huge room without looking back.

'Everyone ... I'd like you to meet Skye Silver. She and I have been *involved* recently.'

'A little subtlety would be nice,' Skye muttered but had no time to complain further about his introduction because she was immediately surrounded by men and women, who were eager to introduce themselves. After they said their name, they kissed her on the cheek and walked away. It was the oddest experience Skye had ever had. It was like some form of initiation that she didn't understand.

The evening passed by in a haze after that. Skye accepted a glass of wine from Tadeo and she found herself enjoying the company of his unusual friends. She even spoke to a woman who looked a lot like the one she had seen in the painting in the parlour. For the first time Skye was curious about Tadeo beyond her sexual fascination with him.

As the last of the guests dispersed Skye stood in the doorway of the entertaining room and watched Tadeo close the front door. It was difficult to imagine that just a few hours ago she had entered this house for the first time, knowing nothing about his life outside of their relationship.

'This is your house, isn't it?' she said.

'Yes. I run the Bastet Society.'

'And what exactly is the Bas ... tet Society?'

'An ancient religion you might say,' Tadeo said. 'The ancient Egyptians worshiped Bastet. She was a beautiful cat goddess.'

'You don't seem the religious type,' Skye said. 'Let alone someone who would run a cult.'

'We prefer society or religion to cult. *That* word has been associated with many strange faiths. Ours is a meeting of like-minded people. We believe in one Goddess; just as western culture believes in one God.'

'I'm tired,' Skye said. 'Could you call a cab for me?'

'I thought you might stay the night,' Tadeo said.

'I have work tomorrow,' she lied.

Tadeo stared at Skye for a moment. He appeared to be on the brink of responding. Perhaps he was even going to beg her to stay. Skye wondered how she might feel if he showed any desperation.

A black tuxedo cat slinked into the room distracting them both from a potentially awkward moment. Skye bent to stroke the cat.

'Where have you been hiding?' she said as the cat rubbed itself against her hand.

'Sebastian doesn't like crowds,' Tadeo explained.

'Oh! He has the same name as your friend. Where did *that* Sebastian go? I didn't see him again.'

'The only Sebastian in this house this evening was this one,' Tadeo said.

Skye's head began to hurt as she looked down at the cat. He appeared to be grinning back up at Tadeo, as though the cat and the human shared a private joke.

'I need some sleep,' Skye said. 'I'll catch a cab outside.'

'Skye?' said Tadeo.

'Yes?'

'Did you *like* my friends?'

'The evening was a bit … odd. I'm not sure what to think.'

Without waiting for his response Skye let herself out of the house and walked down the steps. She had seen a side of Tadeo that she had never wanted to see. He was successful, rich and he ran a cat cult. It was all just a bit flaky and weird for her liking.

The kink of Tadeo biting the back of her neck as he rode her from behind now made sense. She really didn't want to make the association beyond their actual fucking … But he did have a thing for cats …

*I have lousy luck with men. Why couldn't he have a normal*

*job? A delivery guy, or taxi driver …*

The evening had raised more questions about Tadeo than she wanted answers for. To get those answers would mean more commitment and allowing their relationship to grow. Skye didn't want that. Commitment was something she had never done. She liked the idea even less now that she knew more about Tadeo. What kind of *man* ran a 'society' that worshiped cats? It was just too creepy.

She glanced around the quiet street. She would have to make her way back to a main road in order to find a black cab. She glanced at her watch, it was two in the morning, and the tube service ended at midnight and didn't restart until about five. She would have to foot the bill for the cab fare all the way home.

She felt a tinge of resentment that he had expected her to stay in that disturbing house, with those old paintings and a cat that leered at you with crafty intelligence.

Skye pulled her mind back to the moment. She glanced back at Tadeo's house. It was in complete darkness now, blacked out and empty-looking. As though no one lived there. She walked away, down to the end of the street, and glanced down to the junction beyond. The roads were quite empty. Skye had never been out this late alone before. Late nights were spent with girlfriends in nightclubs, picking up the occasional casual fling, or eating alone, with a bottle of Jack for company. She glanced back down Tadeo's street; the house stood out by its sheer lack of any light. Even the streetlight shunned it, casting its light in a sideways glow towards the road and away from the pavement.

'My imagination is running away with me,' she murmured. The sound of her whispered words carried into the night. It chilled her to the bone.

Skye hurried on towards the junction because it was the most likely place to find a cab.

*I could have stayed a few more hours at his house,* she thought, regretting the decision to leave. *Only three more hours until the tube station reopens after all!*

A cat hissed from the steps of a house as she passed. Skye jumped and then glared at the creature as it stared at her from the shadows, eyes reflecting the streetlamps, revealing its position.

'Stupid cat!' she said.

At that moment a black cab turned the corner and headed towards her . The 'for hire' light was on.

'Thank God! Taxi!'

She waved her arms and the cab driver saw her and drew into the curb.

'Where to Miss?'

Skye moved through the dark hallway towards her lounge door. There was a glow coming from the room through the partial crack of the door. She must have left her lamp on before leaving the evening before and she was now grateful to see that warm light welcoming her home.

'What are you doing here?' she said. Her voice trembled.

Tadeo was sitting on her two-seater sofa: this was freaky, even for him.

'Sit down,' Tadeo said. 'I've something important to tell you.'

When Tadeo stopped talking Skye ran a hand over her forehead. She was tired, drained and concerned that the man was a complete stalker and nutcase.

'I know it's difficult to take in,' he continued. 'But every few hundred years Bastet is reincarnated, and I am always there to facilitate it.'

A feeling of *déjà vu* made Skye feel dizzy. She felt she had heard these words before, but didn't know when or how.

'I'm too tired for this shit tonight. This has all been some freaky game to you, hasn't it? And. It's not funny. I need to sleep and I want you to leave.'

'The process has already begun,' Tadeo said. 'At the initiation this evening.'

'What are you talking about?'

'The cats accepted you. And you accepted their kiss.'

Skye's mind wobbled between the memory she thought she had and the idea that Tadeo's words conjured up. In a flashback, she saw herself accepting the rough-tongued lick of one cat after another, ending with the one called Sebastian.

'That's what really happened today,' Tadeo said, reading her mind.' You met the family.'

Skye slumped back into her chair. She was exhausted and couldn't think straight. His insane words rang in her head.

*You are Bastet. You will remember your calling.*

She woke in an unfamiliar bed. A large four-poster, with thick drapes hanging from each corner. There was an old-style lamp beside the bed. Skye saw the antique furnishings, beautifully preserved objects, and knew that she was back in the Hammersmith house. Maybe she had stayed here after all and everything else had been a dream.

The lamp beside the bed contained a candle shaped bulb that made it appear to be a real flame, and not electrical lighting.

Skye slid from the bed and caught sight of herself in a full-length mirror that stood beside the wardrobe. Hammer horror movie female – victim or seductress? She could be dressed as either. She was wearing a long, sheer nightgown with a plunging neckline which accentuated her small breasts.

*What was I drinking last night?*

She went to the window, pulled back the corner of one drape and looked out. The street was still dark, dawn appeared to be hours away. If anything, by the movement of people and traffic outside, Skye would place the time at around eight at night. But which night?

She glanced at her wrist but her watch was gone. Of course it was! Along with her own clothing, which another quick look around the room revealed was nowhere in sight.

She sighed. Tadeo and his games ...

She found a white robe thrown over a chair and she pulled it on over the nightdress. It had long mediaeval style sleeves and a hood – probably some sexual fantasy of Tadeo's. She smirked but it was humourless.

Tying the robe belt securely around her waist she left the room.

Downstairs she heard a regular ticking and noticed an old grandfather clock by the door. She hadn't noticed it before, but didn't worry too much about it as she looked at the time. It was eleven thirty, later than she had guessed it was.

She tried to open the front door to look outside, but discovered it was locked. There was a mortise lock and no key. Perturbed, she walked down the corridor and began opening doors to see what was inside each room. On one side she saw the doors to the entertaining room. She knew that this big space stretched from the front of the house and most of the way back. On the other side there was the parlor, a study, and the third door led to a short corridor presumably towards the kitchen which was sited at the back of the house. There was also a door under the wide staircase that she hadn't previously noticed.

'Tadeo?' she called.

It didn't surprise her that there was no reply. The house was a vacuum, devoid of human presence other than her own.

She braved the corridor to the kitchen but then a noise behind her drew her back to the hallway.

The door under the stairs was now open. The flickering of candles reflected on the walls of a stairwell and cast shadows into the hallway.

'Tadeo?' she said again, but his name came out as a mere whisper.

Skye was drawn to the door, legs moving despite the feeling that she really wanted to run in the opposite direction. She passed over the threshold as though floating. She was unable to stop herself.

A wooden staircase wound downwards, curving left. Skye followed and walked down for what felt like an impossibly long time. Every few steps she encountered a well in the side of the wall, with a lit candle nestled inside. This was the light for the stairway and it was sufficient and atmospheric. Eventually the wooden steps gave way to concrete, leading ever downwards.

*Okay, so he's into even more kinky shit than I realized,* Skye thought. *Perhaps this will be fun ...*

The stairwell opened out onto a short platform, and then the stairs curved down in the opposite direction. Skye had no concept of how many steps she had already travelled down, but she had the feeling it was many. She had started to count them, but lost count several times in the hypnotic monotony of the descent. Perhaps it was in the region of the steps that led down to the catacombs that she had once visited on a trip to Paris. That was years ago now, and she hadn't enjoyed the experience of dead skulls and bones laid out in artistic patterns in some bizarre Parisian underworld.

She became aware of the change in the steps after the platform. The ones before had been regular concrete, these were now cut stone, ancient, and with worn indentations from the passage of thousands of feet over thousands of years.

Then, with abrupt finality, the steps ended.

Skye was facing a rock wall. There was no basement. The candlelight from the alcove opposite danced over the wall.

'What is this shit?'

Skye reached out and touched the wall in front of her. It was cold but not damp. Then it began to move. The wall slid left, disappearing into the rock at her side.

The radiance from hundreds of candles illuminated a stunning room. The floor and walls were made of polished beige-toned marble, which shone like gold wherever the light fell. There was an unusual pattern carved into the floor. A diamond shape, overlapped by a circle.

Skye looked at the floor markings, and realized that there were symbols and shapes engraved all over it. Symbols that almost formed into words – a language that she didn't understand but seemed to hold meaning for her nonetheless.

'Your parents taught you nothing did they?'

Skye turned to see Tadeo. He was lying on a red velvet

*chaise longue* at the other side of the room. Skye could have sworn that the room had been empty when she entered.

'What would you know about my parents?'

Tadeo sat up and stared at her, his brow furrowed. 'I see. You were adopted. That explains a lot. But not why they gave you up and didn't prepare you for today.'

'I'm not playing your games today, Tadeo. Of course I wasn't adopted!'

'This isn't a game, Skye. This is my destiny. It is what I live for, reincarnation, after reincarnation.'

'Where are my clothes?'

'You'll have new robes once you are transformed ...'

'Okay, I'm out of here ...'

Skye turned back towards the stairs only to find the doorway full of cats, their eyes fixed on her and glinting in the iridescent candlelight.

'Bring her in,' Tadeo said.

Skye saw one cat, Sebastian from its black and white chest, creeping forward. As she watched, the cat stretched out along the marble floor. He was impossibly long. He extended his front paws, fingers grew from the clawed toes, and a fifth, a thumb, broke through fur. Sebastian's transformation from cat to human took no more than a few moments, but in that time, Skye saw the torturous remoulding of flesh, the shrinking back of fur on his body – turning into a black tuxedo suit – and the folding back of ears as human hair and skin replaced fur. Sebastian's face became clean shaven, but Skye knew this was no parlour trick. Sebastian had shape-shifted. Were they Werecats then?

She took a step back from the former cat as Sebastian lifted himself up from the floor onto his back legs. He was very much human now, no one would think otherwise, except that Skye could tell by his eyes that this human form was the unnatural state for Sebastian.

Sebastian grabbed Skye's arm and pulled her into the centre of the circle.

'Let go of me, you dick!' she struggled against his

formidable strength.

Skye became aware of the other transformations as more hands grabbed her. She was pulled down to the ground, stretched out and held and by virtue of her horizontal position she found herself staring upwards.

A blaze of stars scattered the black ceiling of the chamber. A constellation which Skye had no knowledge to identify, and even if she had, this arrangement was not one that current technology had even seen.

'M'Lyhr A'Ranoth sumoni Tadeo,' Tadeo said.

Skye heard the words but could make no sense of them. He repeated the phrase over and over until the stars above began to move. The alignment changed and then Skye could distinguish Earth's solar system.

The first pattern approached, then overlaid the second and like a zoom tool on a computer screen the Earth came into solid focus, with the strange diamond and circle patterns embellishing the planet's surface. The zoom-in continued, and Skye saw London, just like on Google Maps, and then Hammersmith and finally the house she was in.

Her mind made sense of it: it was a giant screen - attached to the ceiling.

The marble room trembled, a crack appeared in the image above Skye's head, and then it opened up. This was no screen, no hoax. Something real and terrifying was happening.

Skye screamed in terror as a shadow came through the cosmic portal.

'Open your eyes,' Tadeo said.

Skye shook her head. She was terrified. Her bladder had turned to mush and she felt the warm damp patch of urine seeping through the robe and nightgown, filling the grooves in the marble floor beneath her.

'Open your eyes and see your god, M'Lyhr A'Ranoth: the Queen of Cats.'

Skye's eyes opened. She cowered in her own puddle, small and frail. The cat-humans that had held her had all fallen back. She stared out from her white fur-covered face not understanding that the entrance of M'Lyhr A'Ranoth had brought about her own transformation.

'There, there,' Tadeo said. He stroked her head and back, and Skye felt the rippling sensation of fur being moved.

She opened her mouth but only a small 'meow' came from her throat. She licked her lips and felt the sharp feline teeth that filled her mouth. Then she flexed her paws, extending the claws. She swiped at Tadeo, leaving a furrow of claw marks across the back of his hand. She jumped away from the circle with a sideways hop, back arched, hissing in terror. Then she came face to face with M'Lyhr A'Ranoth.

The shadow had fleshed out into a black form. Skye slunk back, the creature before her was a giant. A cat's head on a muscular female human body.

The shock once again triggered a transformation, and Skye stretched out, taking on her human form once more. She collapsed down, exhausted as M'Lyhr A'Ranoth approached.

The creature hissed at Skye as she cowered, submissive. Then its giant paw swiped the air, Skye threw her arm over her face to protect her eyes, but the claws didn't tear into her flesh as she expected.

She felt a sting as her flesh was pierced by the tip of one of the creature's claws.

Fire surged into her veins. Skye looked down at her arm and saw a black line burning through her flesh. Her skin blackened as it burnt from the inside out. She screamed.

As the cosmos realigned, Tadeo kneeled before the throne.

Bastet was in her rightful place. The transformation from good soul, to pure evil, had once more been achieved.

On the outside Bastet resembled M'Lyhr A'Ranoth, for she was remade in the cat god's own image. Inside she burned, the last vestiges of the personality of Skye were steeped in agony. For no deal with an outer god was ever painless.

Tadeo hoped that this reincarnation would last longer than the previous one. There was only so much pain a cat could endure before completely losing its mind. And once Bastet was lost, her power would fail the society too.

Tadeo bowed his head in supplication.

Fire burned through Skye's body as the power of M'Lyhr A'Ranoth coursed through her. Her skin and hair had turned black as the ancient goddess took possession of her. She screamed in her own mind as the pain washed over and through her soul, tearing her apart. But then … it subsided.

Skye felt control returning to her. The ancient and unknowable presence of the cat goddess was receding …

Skye shuddered and drew in a deep breath. She still had control of the power, but the alien presence was being shed. She opened her eyes and saw Tadao kneeling before her. She looked down at her arm which was rippling with colours like the skin of a tone-changing squid, the blackness faded and changed to brown and then caramel, then white as Skye's unique pigmentation threw off the blackness of the alien and reasserted itself. Colour had never stuck to her before, so why should it now?

As the darkness retreated, so Skye felt the pain lessen until there was nothing but power, nothing but herself. Skye. Bastet. What did it matter what they called her? She was the queen of the cats and now ruler of this little moment in space and time.

She laughed and looked down at Tadao. Reaching out one hand/paw she lifted his head by his chin to look at him. Her eyes sparkled blue and bronze, flecked with green and a hint of darkness as her slitted irises observed that the man was scared of her. And so he should be. For she was Bastet, and he was her toy, her plaything.

The other cats had backed away and were scurrying back up the long staircase to the world above. Taking the message. Letting the world know.

Bastet was back!

# The Cuban Curse

*Cuba, September 1st 1933*

'Come in,' said a female voice.

Rolon walked into the darkened room and it took a moment for his eyes to adjust to the gloom. In the far corner a woman sat on the other side of a round table. He could tell she was facing him, even though a heavy scarf was draped over her hair, and covered her eyes as she looked down at a huge diamond.

'Sit,' she said.

Rolon was nervous, he had never been to see a *bruja* before and he wasn't sure, even now though he was desperate for help, that it was such a good idea.

'I'm no witch,' the woman said as Rolon took the seat opposite her.

'I didn't say you …' Rolon was startled, he wondered if he had somehow spoken his thoughts aloud.

'Names are important to my people. I'm Seleste,' she said. 'Which means I have more affiliation with the celestial, than with any demon realms. And you are Rolon. Named so after the wolf of our Spanish conquerors.'

Seleste looked up. Rolon shrank back into his chair, not because Seleste was ugly, warted, a wizened crone as he might have expected, but because she was incredibly beautiful. She had the golden coloured skin of any local, but her eyes glittered amber: the exact colour of a cat that Rolon had once fed scraps to in the street when he was a boy growing up in Havana.

'Forgive me,' Rolon said.

'You expected me to be very different,' Seleste said and there was a gleam in her eye that made Rolon realise that he had not, as he feared, offended her. He had in fact behaved exactly as she had expected him to do.

'Yes,' he said. 'I did not expect a wise woman to be so young ...'

Seleste half smiled. She turned her gaze back down to the gem on her table. This close Rolon could see that the jewel was indeed a diamond and it was wider than his palm; an incredibly valuable stone.

'This gem has been in my family for centuries,' Seleste said, 'passed down from mother to daughter. It was given to us by a Spanish officer. A reward for sparing his life.'

'Sparing his life how?' asked Rolon.

Seleste's cat-like eyes met Rolon's gaze.

'I'm descended from the *Taino*. Hatuey was my ancestor. He was an early revolutionary.'

'He was killed by the Spanish ...' Rolon said, and he remembered the tale from his childhood, of how the Chief of the Taino tried to fight Diego Velázquez de Cuéllar and his men when they first tried to take Cuba. Later, Hatuey was burnt at the stake, something, Rolon noted now, that was often done to those they suspected of witchcraft.

It was strange that Seleste brought this up now, when he, Rolon, was considering following Fulgencio Batista y Zaldívar, his Sergeant, into a coup against their superiors. A coup that could cost him his life, or change everything for the Cuban people, depending on how it went. Rolon had been ready to follow Batista, but then, his sister's husband died, leaving her with two small children and no one but Rolon to take care of her. The wolf-fire inside him that raged against the country's politics was quelled. Rolon no longer felt he could risk court martial, with a possibility of execution, if the revolt failed. He couldn't leave gentle Palmira with no protection. What would happen to her and the children?

'I need protection ...' Rolon said.

'Yes,' Seleste said. 'You do. But not from the thing you most fear.'

'I cannot tell you more, other than I am torn between a decision that could help many and one that can help my sister.'

'A difficult dilemma. But again, I say to you. This thing does not matter. The revolution will be successful. All will work out and Cuba will be better for it,' Seleste said.

Rolon drew in a breath. *How could she know so much?*

She was smiling at him again, watching him like a sleepy cat watches a fish swimming in a bowl.

He turned his eyes down to the diamond. What had she seen in there?

'The future is set and your decision does not matter,' Seleste said again. Then she covered up the diamond with a blood red cloth. The meeting was over.

Knowing he was dismissed, Rolon stood and turned towards the door.

'But what if ...' he said turning back.

The chair was empty, the table devoid of cloth or precious jewel. Seleste had gone. A parlour trick, no doubt.

Rolon shrugged and left the room, walking now back into the bar. The backroom door closed on him.

'What did she say?' asked Guillermo.

'The future is already decided. No decision we make will change it.'

Guillermo laughed. 'Witches hey. They are all whores in the end.'

'Not her,' said Rolon. He glanced back at the door and then towards the drink that his friend held up to him. 'No. We must have an early night. Tomorrow we take our country back.'

Rolon walked away from the bar and out into the street, then he made his way back down the dark streets towards Palmira's house.

It was late, but a welcoming light still shone in the window of the small house as Rolon approached. He tapped lightly on the door and soon Palmira opened it, stepped back to allow him into the confined space.

The house was as many were in the town, small and cramped. Rolon felt a momentary claustrophobia as he entered the tiny living space that served as both living room and kitchen. Out back, in a yard was a filthy outhouse, and upstairs the one room that housed the pallet beds of his sister and her two children.

Even now, long after his death, Rolon cursed his former brother-in-law. He had brought nothing but poverty and squalor to his sister. Then, through reckless behaviour, had foolishly got himself killed in a bar fight. The man had been a drunk, a womaniser, a wastrel. What had his sweet natured sister ever seen in him, beyond his once rakish looks?

'How are you this evening?' he asked now.

'Good. I was offered work today. In the bakery. So soon I will be able to feed my family myself, and have no need to take more of your hard-earned soldiering money.'

'Forget the bakery. Why not move back to the farm? Living in the city is enough to destroy a man's soul.'

'What do you know about it? Living in barracks as you do?'

Rolon sighed. Palmira could be so stubborn. Just like their mother had been. 'The farm needs a housekeeper. You could earn your independence taking care of our childhood home. No one knows the running of that place better than you …' he said

Palmira shook her head. 'Our life is here …'

'But what kind of life can you expect for your son and daughter living like this? The farm house is big. There is good land for the children to grow and play. Remember how we always could roam free and safe?'

'Yes. I remember.'

'I'm not asking you to accept charity. It's a job. I need someone to take care of things while I'm on duty.'

'You are being sent away?' Palmira asked sharply. Her eyes glittered with unshed tears. For all of her brave words she did appreciate Rolon's care: feared his absence and possible death.

'I'll send a carriage to move you out of town. It will be safe for you there.'

'What aren't you telling me?' she said.

'Just that … something big is about to happen.'

Palmira was quiet for a moment and then she nodded. 'Okay. We'll be ready. First thing.'

'Good,' said Rolon. 'And now I must return to barracks. I'll arrange the carriage on the way. Be ready by dawn.'

Rolon slipped away through the narrow door, feeling for the

first time in a while, that his sister's condition was soon to be drastically improved. Now he could put her from his mind and do as his leader wanted. Tomorrow they would attack, and while the government fell, Palmira and her children would be whisked to safety.

In the days that followed, Rolon had no time to think about Palmira or the children, but the carriage he had hired had returned, sending a note that told him she was safe. The country was in upheaval, but changes were being wrought and those corrupt individuals that had ruled his land were now no longer in power. He forgot too that the *bruja* had said all would be fine. That they would win and Cuba would be better for it.

Then, when the world was righting itself, and Rolon could relax once more he saw the witch again.

A ball was held in honour of Fulgencio Batista y Zaldívar and his men, and Rolon, as one of his personal bodyguards, was of course asked to go.

There was a strange mix of people at the ball. Some were the aristocracy who had chosen to fall in with Fulgencio: now they wined and dined the man they once looked down on. Others were the wives and girlfriends of the soldiers attending, and they were ordinary folk, in an extraordinary situation.

Rolan was working the room; he was suspicious of the aristocrats, not as convinced by their friendship as his superiors appeared to be. Fulgencio was over in the far corner of the room, surrounded by a group of men that consisted of soldiers and aristos. For the time being Rolan felt his idol to be safe enough to take his eyes from him. He looked around the room, taking in the small clusters of people. Some he knew well, others not at all. Then his eyes fell on a dark-haired beauty.

Out of the setting in which he had first seen her, Rolon did not immediately recognise Seleste. It was her cat-like eyes, and the soft movement of her lips as they turned up in a smile of greeting.

Rolon was taken aback to see the girl there. She appeared younger still than their first meeting. Barely a woman, and yet he had thought her to be in her mid-twenties.

He found himself moving towards her, weaving through the crowd. He lost sight of her as a soldier and his wife walked between them and then, as he skirted around the couple, he discovered Seleste was gone.

'Dear friend,' said a voice beside him. 'What has you hurrying?'

Rolon turned to see Guillermo with a pretty woman who he knew to be the wife of another soldier.

'I'm keeping Senora Calista company. Will you join us?'

Rolon did not want to offend Guillermo, or the senora and so he paused and passed a few words with them.

'How is your husband?' he asked.

Senora Calista smiled and nodded her head to the group standing with Fulgencio. 'Happy,' she said. 'I feared the worst when this thing began, but now look at us. We've never been stronger. I have such hopes now for the future of our child.'

As she spoke, she subconsciously stroked her stomach and Rolon's eyes skitted politely away from the small bulge he saw there.

After that he excused himself and went in search of Seleste. He had to find her. It was a compulsion he couldn't resist.

He found her outside. She was standing in the gardens of the house gazing out over a rolling garden, with a pool of water decorously placed in the centre.

'Our world is changing,' Seleste said. 'There are those who would make even further changes.'

'You were right,' he said. 'We succeeded in our endeavours.'

Seleste didn't look at him. She continued to gaze at the water.

'There is evil afoot, Rolon,' she said. 'Evil that a man like you can fight ... and triumph over. If you are brave enough.'

'Perhaps you already know the answer to that,' he said.

Seleste glanced at him then. And he was taken aback by the amber eyes once more, there was a cat-like sly tilt that gave her a wary intelligence. And something else, she was smaller in height now than he remembered, and appeared to be a child of no more than 11 years old.

'How can this be?' he asked.

'What you see is the truth. I've been here before and after. And in some future of my own but a past of yours, we met and I gave you the advice you needed.'

'Then how do you know who I am now?'

'I've always known you. Do you remember the advice I gave you?'

'You said the future was set.'

Seleste smiled. 'It is.'

'Then what is the point of getting any advice?'

'There are moments when the future is still being decided. These are usually before you know you need to make a decision. At such times, the outcome can be changed.'

Rolon frowned. He wasn't sure what Seleste meant, all he could focus on was her youth. How would someone so young know anything?

'How can you know this?'

'Come and see me again …' she said.

Then in the blink of an eye, she vanished.

When she was gone, Rolon stared at the place she had once occupied and then, confused and more than a little afraid, he crossed himself and went back inside.

For weeks Rolon tried not to think about Seleste and consciously refused to see her. But his sleep became erratic, and dreams of the girl, beautiful no matter what age, haunted him until, unable to resist her call, he finally went back to the tavern.

It was an unusually quiet night. The celebrations following the revolution had stopped and the everyday life, out of necessity, was normalising. Sometimes, Rolon wondered if the people were any better off at all. Nothing much had changed, other than the people in charge, but Rome wasn't built in a day, and his superiors advised that the changes would happen, if slowly at first.

'She's waiting for you ...' said the tavern keeper. He nodded his head toward the door at the back.

As Rolon approached, the door opened and he paused at the threshold.

'Why do you hesitate?' Seleste's voice carried to him. He peered into the darkness of the room but could see nothing.

'Cross,' she prompted.

Rolon put one foot forward into the room and then found himself sat opposite Seleste and the huge diamond once more.

He glanced over his shoulder at the door back to the tavern, confused. He had no memory of walking in and sitting down.

'You came of your own free will,' Seleste said.

He looked at her now. Older than the last time her saw her, but younger than the first.

'How can this be?' he asked.

'Time is subjective,' Seleste explained. 'It depends when you enter the stream and when you leave.'

'Stream,' Rolon said. 'I don't know why I'm here ...'

Seleste smiled. '*I* summoned you.'

Her hand was on his now. A warmth grew in the place where their skin touched.

'I need you Rolon.'

Rolon found himself lost in Seleste's amber eyes. They no longer looked human and there were more of them than the original too.

'I need more babies,' Seleste said but the sound came from somewhere other than her small pale pink lips.

Rolon tried to pull back: there was a blurred and disgusting mass before him, with multiple eyes, and several small winged creatures attached to it. Suckling like desperate babies starved of a mother's precious milk. A snake like appendage gripped his arm. He felt numb, even his emotions were dampened, and this horrific thing brought nothing to him other than a vague confusion.

'Where is Seleste?' he said.

'Through time and space, I see all. You will give me more

children.'

Once more Rolon tried to pull away, but the creature had his arm and it would not let go. Panic seeped into the numbness now.

'Let me go!' he gasped.

'Not until you give me what I want ...'

There was a cruel guttural laughter then. Rolon heaved and tugged until his arm ached in his shoulder and then the darkness swooped in and he thought no more.

It took Rolon a few moments to come around. His cheek was pressed to the hard, wooden surface of a table. He could feel the intense heat of a fire at his back. His head was foggy, as though he were waking following an intense drinking session on a night out of the barracks. He flexed his fingers, felt the pain of pins and needles in his arms and then he pushed himself up into a sitting position.

He cast watery eyes over the room. He was in the main bar of the tavern. He didn't remember coming back in here. On the table in front of him was a half-filled flagon of ale and a tankard. Rolon's mouth was dry and so he poured some of the ale and drank it down in one long gulp.

He thought he heard the flapping of wings and he turned sharply and looked behind him. The place was almost empty. A few prostitutes were hanging around the bar drinking. Two old men we sat by the fire and a young, but crippled, soldier sat alone near the door as though he were waiting to be called to arms again.

Rolon pressed a hand against his head. He didn't know how he had got here. Why had he come to the tavern initially? There was a heavy feeling around his head and his arm hurt, as though he'd somehow been trapped and held by something incredibly strong.

A flash of memory brought goosebumps to the back of his neck. A humanoid mass, a thing with protruding amber eyes and then, those wings, flapping and that appendage that gripped and pulled him towards …

'No …' Rolon gasped.

It was a drink-crazed dream nothing more …

His hand was shaking as he poured more ale into the tankard and then Rolon saw the awful state of his forearm, covered as it was in small pinprick marks as though a plague of mosquitos had descended on him.

Rolon staggered from the tavern and headed back to the barracks. His mind awash with flashbacks of horror. By the time he arrived Rolon was in a state of shock. He believed that something awful had happened to him. But he couldn't remember what it was. He fell to his bed. His arm hurt, his mind was fragmented and he was slowly starting to believe that somehow, he had been violated.

Though the details of this assault were vague and distant, and still horrifically nightmarish, Rolon knew the link was Seleste. He saw her now in her glorious beauty, amber eyes glowing with an intelligent fire. How did she know about the future? What was she? Then he remembered she was Taino …

Exhausted and drained, Rolon slept.

The next day, Rolon could barely rouse himself for roll call and as he stumbled from his bunk, pulling on his uniform, he realised with horror that his arm was no longer what it used to be.

He let out a frightened yell.

'What happened to you?' asked Guillermo.

Rolon held out his arm and Guillermo backed away as he saw the withered appendage that protruded from his friend's uniform.

'It's the curse,' he said. 'The Cuban curse. Maybe we'll all get it!'

'No … ' Rolon said. 'That witch she …'

'What witch?' Guillermo asked.

'The one from the tavern …'

Guillermo took Rolon's good arm and pulled him from the

barracks. 'You went back to see her?' he said. 'If she's cursed you. We'll force her to remove it.'

Rolon let Guillermo lead him back to the tavern. As they entered, Rolon felt a renewal of his own strength.

'There. She works from the back room,' Rolon said.

'Only whores work in these places,' Guillermo said and Rolon remembered that his friend had called Seleste a whore the first time too. For some reason his disrespect of the girl was important. Rolon didn't understand why, and he did not defend Seleste this time. She had done something to him. She was not who she had seemed.

Guillermo walked to the door that Rolon indicated and opened it. Inside was a small storage cupboard. He turned and looked at Rolon.

'There's nothing here.'

Rolon came forward and stared into the cupboard. 'I don't understand. She's always been there. This isn't the room then. I must be mistaken.'

But they looked around the tavern and found no other rooms on the lower floor that fitted the description Rolon gave.

Rolon's withered arm began to throb and burn.

'You need to see a doctor,' Guillermo said. 'That could be diseased. Contagious.'

By then Rolon was in so much discomfort he was unable to argue.

They entered the apothecary shop some time later.

'My friend needs help,' Guillermo said to the small man behind the counter. 'He needs a doctor. Or something ...'

The man offered Rolon a chair. By then Rolon's face was ashen and he was clutching his arm as though he expected it to fall off at any moment.

The apothecary pulled back the sleeve of Rolon's uniform and looked down at the appendage.

'I have never seen the like. How long has he been like this?'

'A few hours,' Guillermo said, because Rolon was in such pain he could barely speak.

'Help me get him into the back room. I know who to send for …' said the apothecary. 'An expert in … unusual sickness.'

Rolon could barely walk now, and the two men half carried, half dragged, the soldier into the back room. There was a pallet and the apothecary and Guillermo laid Rolon down.

'I can give him something for the pain,' said the apothecary. 'Laudanum …'

Guillermo nodded. 'Hurry. He looks like he might lose his mind.'

Rolon drifted in a drug induced sleep, his mind split from the pain in his arm as it became a distant ache. Guillermo helped the apothecary remove Rolon's shirt and they laid him back on the pallet, making him as comfortable as possible.

'I've sent my son to get help,' the apothecary said and then he put another drop of laudanum in water and fed it to the dazed patient.

The bell on the front door rang, and the apothecary left Rolon and Guillermo as he went into the shop.

'This way,' Guillermo heard him say.

Then, he entered with a tall woman. She wore a cloak. The hood hid her face from Guillermo. She went straight to the pallet and looked at Rolon.

'Oh no!' she gasped. 'I told him to come and see me. But he never came. This could have been prevented.'

'Who are you?' Guillermo said.

She dropped her hood and looked at the young soldier. Guillermo was struck by the beauty of her face and the incredible glow of her amber coloured eyes. 'I'm Seleste. I tried to warn your friend.'

'Warn him of what?'

Seleste sighed. 'There is a breach in time and space. Sometimes *it* seeps through.'

'You're the witch he told me of. You did this to him!'

Guillermo grabbed Seleste's arm, but with a shrug she threw the young man off. Guillermo had no urge to grab her again. He knew such behaviour would be a terrible mistake.

'I didn't do this. Though it may have used my image in its seduction.'

'Who then?' Guillermo said.

'It goes by many names, the most common … Yibb-Tsll. It is a creature who sees through and beyond space and time. As I do. But I do not abuse my power.'

'What has it done to him?'

'Your friend has become food for the creature. It took something from him and now his vitality is being bled away by this creature's unholy offspring. Unless we break the link, Rolon will die.'

'How do we save him?' Guillermo asked.

Seleste didn't speak for a moment. She closed her eyes and stood perfectly still as though she were praying for the answer. When she opened her eyes again, Guillermo understood his friend's obsession with her. She was compelling, drawing Guillermo into her intrigue, as surely as she had Rolon.

'We must close the breach. If we do this, Yibb-Tsll will no longer be able to sustain its connection to Rolon. He is a good man and does not deserve to die before his time.'

'I'll help you,' said Guillermo. 'But how do we close this … breach?'

'Someone is corrupt …'

'Corrupt in what way?'

'They must have access to a necronomicon. A powerful grimoire with spells to open the way for the Old Ones to come through to our world.'

'I don't understand you, girl,' Guillermo said. 'But I'll help you anyway. What must I do?'

'I must give Rolon some protection. If Yibb-Tsll realises our plan it will try to take all of him quickly. Then, you must come with me. It will take two of us to do what is needed.'

The apothecary brought in a wand of lit sage and Seleste stepped back and watched as he waved the sage over Rolon.

There was a strong odour, but the air appeared cleaner for it. And then Seleste began to chant in a language that Guillermo had never heard. When she stopped speaking Rolon became restless. At that point, the apothecary waved the sage over his body once more.

'His arm!' Guillermo said. 'I think it's improving.'

Seleste began her chant once more, and this time, when she finished, Rolon fell into a deep and restful sleep.

'I've blocked the connection, but the barrier won't last long. We need to find the source of the breach. Where did Rolon meet with the creature?'

Guillermo explained about the tavern.

'He said he met you there initially. But the room didn't exist.'

'I did meet him there, in a space between worlds. Yibb-Tsll has found an entry point into that space. But it is only possible if someone helped the creature by chanting the right spell. I suspect it may be the landlord.'

'What must we do?' Guillermo asked.

'We need to close the portal,' Seleste said, 'and stop the landlord – if it is him – from reopening it. For that I will need your strength Guillermo.'

Guillermo wondered how Seleste had known his name. He didn't recall telling it to her.

'Where is the landlord?' asked Seleste. There was a young barmaid behind the bar of the tavern.

'Upstairs,' the girl said. 'But he's with one of the girls right now. I don't think he'll be happy to be disturbed.'

'We'll deal with him later,' said Seleste.

They went to the door that Rolon had said he had entered and as they reached it a peculiar sensation ran over Guillermo's skin, making the hairs on his arms and the back of his neck stand up. Guillermo shuddered and Seleste looked at him sharply.

'You feel that?' she said.

He nodded, his heart racing. He was almost too afraid to

speak.

Seleste stepped forward then and touched the door. It sprang open and then Guillermo saw the space that Rolon had entered - not the storage room that Guillermo had seen on their last visit, but a proper room.

There was a howling wind inside, as though the very fabric of the universe had been ripped open, and it pulled at Guillermo as he stood on the threshold.

'What do we do now?' Guillermo asked.

'I have to do something. Remain there,' Seleste said.

Guillermo's eyes were drawn into the room and he barely acknowledged Seleste as he saw the creature for the first time.

It was dark inside the room but Guillermo could make out Yibb-Tsll in the farthest corner. The creature was humanoid in shape, but that was where the similarity to humanity ended. It had numerous eyes, too many to count, and huge black wings that spread the width of the room. It's mass writhed, as though it was covered in heaving pustules. Guillermo couldn't turn away from the monstrosity, he felt himself drawn forward but resisted. And then he saw what was really moving on the creature. Hundreds, possibly thousands of small vampiric creatures that bit and suckled on its blackened flesh. The creature writhed as though it was the most pleasurable experience.

'My god,' Guillermo gasped.

'Yes,' said Seleste behind him. 'Yibb-Tsll is a god of sorts. An ancient deity and she requires a sacrifice before she will release your friend.'

'A sacrifice?' Guillermo said. 'What do we give it?'

'You ...' said Seleste.

Then she began to chant again. That abstract and guttural language that he'd heard her use on Rolon, and Guillermo could no longer resist the pull of the air and he stepped over the threshold.

The air was sucked from his lungs as he was caught up by a huge appendage and pulled forward. Yibb-Tsll cried out a guttural laugh, but Guillermo could not see the mouth from which it came. He saw instead the hideous creatures, lifting off from the bulk of their mother and swarming instead around him. Tiny teeth ripped and tore at any exposed flesh, and then he felt his uniform pulled away.

Guillermo breathed in, trying to fill his lungs enough to scream his horror. The air, however, was a vacuum. And no matter how hard he tried he could not call for help.

Somewhere distant he heard Seleste chanting and then the vampiric creatures descended on his naked body. His arms were pulled wide and they bit into and suckled on his flesh and blood as though he were a mother with a thousand nipples and every part of his body, even his penis, was latched onto.

Inside his head, Guillermo screamed.

He was driven completely insane before his drained body dropped dead to the floor of the portal room.

Seleste closed the door of the room, symbolically closing the portal, and locking Yibb-Tsll out. The sight of Guillermo dying would remain with her but there had been no other solution. She had to save Rolon.

For, like her mother Yibb-Tsll, Seleste could see all of space and time. Rolon's future was important: he would become the father of a generation of new deities, while she would be the mother. It was a huge burden on them both.

Back in the bar the landlord waited for her. He held out the book, wrapped in the same blood red cloth that had once been used to cover the diamond Seleste used to focus her vision on the future.

She took the book, muttering a few words that would erase the landlord's memory of her, the necronomicon and of Rolon and Guillermo.

Seleste left the tavern and made her way back to the apothecary shop. There she would find Rolon much recovered and grateful. Then her work on him would really begin.

# Breaking Point

Kerys and Mai huddled down behind the remaining dried husks of trees and watched as a group of men loitered by the rusting slide. They were smoking something. It might have been the remnants of tobacco-filled cigarettes, difficult to find, or some of the new stuff that was favoured among the scavengers because of its hallucinogenic properties. Kerys didn't know. She didn't care. All she cared about was that she and Mai weren't seen.

These were dark days. The end of all eras. A fall from grace that could never be rectified. A cold and vicious wind swept through the deserted land. All signs of life were fading, as trees shrivelled from their roots upwards, weeds no longer thrived unchecked and the patches of grass look like dried, charred wasteland.

In what used to be a children's playground a dried bush, ripped out by the roots, rolled with the airstream like tumbleweed. Dull clouds loomed overhead. There was an absence of noise. The world was afraid to speak, even the wind's whistle was subdued as though it were scared to draw any attention to itself.

The swings nearby creaked gently in the breeze. The roundabout had long since rusted, unmoveable, and the slide was caked in filth - ash and acid rain that fell intermittently from the poison filled sky.

Kerys and Mai had ventured out from what had been a safe hidey hole down by the docks. It was early morning, though the light remained dimmed. The need for food had pushed away their natural fear of the outside. It wasn't just the cold, harsh weather, or the days that never quite got light, it was the *others* they feared the most.

'What should we ...' Mai began.

'Shush ...' Kerys cautioned.

The wind howled around and through the woodland as though attempting to reveal their hiding place. They couldn't move. To try to leave would reveal their presence, there was nothing they could do but wait.

They didn't have long.

Driven away by the cold the group of men began to shift. Cigarette stubs were dropped, still burning, to the dried and cracked soil. Loud raucous chatter followed them, and it made it easier for Kerys to track their progress as she and Mai lingered.

Patience was something they had learnt the hard way, though the waiting was always difficult, especially when the fear kicked in. And there was always fear. It was on the air, they could taste it in every ash-tainted breath they took, in every mouthful of scavenged food. In every drop of rain that fell.

'Come on,' Kerys said finally.

'But where?' Mai complained.

'That way,' Kerys said, pointing towards the remnants of the town ahead.

'Not there ...' Mai was afraid.

'We have no choice if we want to eat tonight.'

'We could scavenge. That's what others do.'

'We'd have to fight for every morsel. Besides, that's why the scavengers aren't surviving,' Kerys pointed out, 'and we are.'

Kerys hurried across the playground, Mai tried to keep up. Exposed places were always the most difficult when it came to dealing with other scavengers, or worse still, *them*, but it was a risk that was unavoidable.

Hunger clutched at Kerys's stomach, it growled as though it were responding to the wind. As they reached the other side of the open space, Mai gripped her hand and whispered harshly into her ear.

'I can't do it. I'd rather starve than let another of them touch me again.'

'No you wouldn't. You'll do what they want. We both will. Then we can get back and feed the children. If not for ourselves, we'll do this for them.'

Mai fell quiet. She knew what this trip meant more than most. Her pretty, petite figure was always a draw. It was why Kerys brought her along. So few Chinese women had survived. Mai would make good trade, but Kerys would do well too. Perhaps even better than her friend because of her unusual scars. *They* liked to see the damage that had been done by the battle at the end of days. Suffering in any form delighted *them*.

They reached the outskirts of the town unaccosted, then skirted around the edges, avoiding any humans if they saw them. They passed the high street shops with their shattered windows. A food store had its doors ripped from their hinges, the contents long since looted. The streets were full of waste, animal and human, but the animals were less now, as the scavengers caught them for food. The smell was awful.

A roar in the distance brought them both to a halt. One of the Old Ones was out. Hunting down humans to enslave, or kill, it didn't matter which as both meant death in the end.

Mai huddled against the side of the old library building afraid to go on. Kerys took her hand once more. She pulled Mai to her feet. The Old Ones didn't concern them. They had made a deal and they would survive because of it. But first they had to reach the half-breeds.

Kerys and Mai had visited the lair before. It was the journey that was always such a challenge. The half-breeds paid well for what the girls had to offer, and the commune would be able to survive for several weeks on what they would bring back. But it was a horrible thing to face. The prodding, the staring, the couplings that left them bruised and battered. Then that vague moment of what Kerys chose to think of as *kindness* when the girls were given a cart of food to take home.

'Almost there,' Kerys said, but her words were unnecessary.

Mai was shaking so hard that Kerys heard her teeth chatter.

'I won't survive this time,' she said. 'I'm not as strong as you.'

'You will,' Kerys said. 'You have to, or we all die.'

Kerys took her hand. They had reached the entrance. Above

the door was a broken and cracked sign. The name was gone, but the underground symbol still remained. They began their descent down into the bowels of the old tube station.

Kerys let out the breath she had been holding. They were safe now. Outside they could have encountered anything. The Old Ones, the scavengers, or worse still the broken ones. No one ever survived an encounter with them.

They had barely crossed the threshold when Mai squealed. A thick, slimy tentacle had brushed against her bare calf. The playing had already begun.

'You know why we're here,' Kerys said, trying to sound braver than she felt.

The same tentacle brushed across her breasts. She tried not to move. The thing shuffled backwards, she could smell its stink on her though, that awful odour of rot that accompanied the creatures. And although they never spoke, they always seemed to understand the intent of the women. Or maybe, the half-breeds, their masters, could somehow tell them telepathically. Kerys didn't know. It was just one of those mysteries that she often pondered.

They passed down an unmoving escalator. Although there was no electricity, a greenish glow filled the corridors to light their way. Kerys had expected this: *they* didn't want their playthings to injure themselves in the dark. A waft of warm air rushed around them, another testing of the goods probably, but the air stank of the breath exhaled from a rank mouth, that held nothing but rotten, decayed teeth. Kerys forced back the urge to gag, and as she heard Mai begin to heave, she dug her nails into the girl's palm, hard.

'Ouch, why did you …' Mai complained, but soon realised that Kerys had once again taken her mind away from the awful situation.

At the bottom of the escalator the corridor on the right illuminated and the women turned and made their way further down. This one sloped, and it felt as though they were entering the bowels of the Earth.

They reached a former platform. Below, where the tube once

ran at break-neck speed, the tracks were churned up, a hole lay in the centre. Something foul moved inside the hole. Kerys pulled Mai back from the edge as a vicious appendage lashed out towards them.

The women pressed up against the tiled wall keeping back from the crevice as a misty illumination led them onwards towards the side of the platform and down into the tunnel. Kerys glanced back at the hole. She wondered where it led. The centre of the Earth perhaps, or some dark dimension that contained the remnants of the evil that had destroyed and corrupted them.

Mai's hand gripped hers tighter and Kerys could almost feel the hysteria bubbling up inside her friend. The fear was not irrational, even though they had been through this countless times.

Once there had been three of them.

Kerys pushed aside the memory of Amanda but not before the flash of thought delved into her final moment. She barely quelled the sight of Amanda's insides seeping from her torso, as though she were nothing more than a stuffed doll bursting its seams.

'It won't happen to us, will it?' Mai said.

Kerys didn't reply. Ahead of them the old train carriage waited. She saw one of the half-breeds in there, but more would come.

'I'll go first,' Kerys said.

She climbed up into the carriage with Mai at her heels. They could both hear the shift of movement outside as the others were drawn to them, like moths to flames. Only it was the women who were the moths. The half-breeds the flames that would burn them if they weren't careful.

Inside the carriage was a filthy mattress. It was there for the comfort of the girls, not for the monsters who didn't need it. Though Kerys didn't know if these things even slept.

Kerys slipped out of her clothing and lay down on the mattress. She tried not to look at the half-breed - not seeing them made it easier - but the smell was stronger on this one than most. It wasn't just filth, the stench of body odour was something they all lived with, it was something else. Vile, poisonous, they smelt of disease and death. They were like the plague personified.

His appendages explored her, touched the scars. And in her mind she concentrated on that, the puckered flesh was unattractive, but not to these creatures. They liked scar tissue, and this one suckled on it as though he had found an erogenous zone. One of the limbs pushed her legs apart and she lay, accepting the probing, until the thing pushed up inside her, forcing a grunt of pain as it began to move. The thing chuckled in its throat. Giving pain pleased them.

She lay there until it was done, felt the awful flood of its seed filling her, then as it moved away, she stood on shaking limbs. Waiting in the corner, she looked down while another one did the same thing to Mai.

Mai cried though, and she heard the awful titter of pleasure her tears brought to the one abusing her and she felt the excitement of the others waiting in the doorway. The tension in the air made the hairs stand up on her naked skin.

The vile seed slid down her legs, escaping when it failed to work on her, and then she was encouraged onto all fours as another one of them used her. This one grunted like a human man. Kerys kept her eyes closed, forcing herself to imagine that it was only a man after all. The pummelling wasn't as painful as the last one had been and a ripple of excitement flooded her loins as she tried to enjoy it. But the creature didn't want that and so another appendage wrapped around her and pinched one of her nipples hard until she cried out. Her pain brought the half-breed to his climax. Kerys collapsed under the weight of its final thrust.

Standing again she saw Mai, pressed against the window of the train, while a monstrosity pushed itself into her from behind. Through the window she saw several shapes watching. She looked away. How many would they let loose on them until their poor, battered bodies gave them what they needed?

Another picked her up, wrapped her legs around a place

that could have been its waist, she squeezed her eyes closed as it lifted and lowered her on to itself. She couldn't bear to be face to face like this, feeling its hideous breath blowing onto her cheeks.

Outside the carriage a fight broke out. The thing holding her became more excited and finally finished. Its orgasm burnt her insides like hot wax. Her eyes opened to see what the commotion was and she came face to face with it. Snout crumpled, sharp, dangerous teeth gleaming in the dark, the multiple blood shot eyes. It leered at her like a hungry wolf. Bile rose in her throat.

*I won't be sick. They would like that too much.*

Pain and suffering was a drug to them, and they enjoyed human flesh too much, which was why there were so many survivors left alive. Anyone willing to make a deal by selling themselves at least had a chance of survival. The rest would just be picked off one by one by each other or by the gods themselves.

Mai was left to stand in a corner. They waited. Nothing happened. She groaned and sobbed as she was pulled down onto the mattress again.

'Please,' she said.

This brought more laughter, Kerys wished that the girl could just remain silent. She always made it worse for herself by showing so much fear and emotion.

Kerys took her turn in the corner. She could smell the frustration of those still waiting to use her. All hoping that they could continue. It would be such a small thing that would end this for both her and Mai. She hoped that next time would be the last for Mai at least.

One after another they came for them both. Kerys ached from head to toe, Mai cried until her eyes were swollen and then Mai's respite finally came.

In the corner her naked belly twitched and began to swell. One of them had finally impregnated her and the thing inside grew rapidly. Kerys was pushed aside. Mai was placed once more on the mattress until she birthed the thing, a mass of black tentacles that seemed to claw its way out of her, while she screamed with the worst pain yet.

Afterwards another mattress was brought in. They left Mai bleeding, the half-breed was taken from the carriage, and Kerys's torment began again until she, like Mai had given them another monstrosity.

The things backed away from the carriage then, though one brought them some foul cocktail that the women were forced to drink. They knew that it would help them heal somehow and so did not fight. Kerys and Mai were used to this process. After all it had taken place once a month since the beginning of the end.

When they were sufficiently recovered, Kerys got up and began to dress. Mai remained still on the mattress. The birthing always seemed to take more out of her, and the recovery, despite the medicine, was slower than for Kerys.

'Come on Mai, we need to get back,' Kerys said.

Mai didn't answer.

Kerys pulled her tee-shirt over her head, then she went to the second mattress. She was sore, but healing rapidly. It was a shame that they didn't know what the potion was, it could, possibly, help them all heal from other injuries.

Mai turned her head towards the window. Kerys glanced there, saw that some of the creatures were still lurking. Perhaps these ones would be first in line next time. But they were safe for now, and they would be allowed to leave as easily as they had entered. Those had always been the rules.

Kerys helped Mai dress – she was slowly recovering her faculties. By the time Kerys pulled on her shoes, Mai was fit to leave.

'Let's go,' Kerys said, supporting Mai with an arm around her waist. They struggled back through the corridors and up the escalator. At the entrance they found the cart. It held cans of all sorts of food, some half rotten vegetables, and a few bottles of water, cola and lemonade.

In the shadows, scavengers shrank back, allowing them to pass. Kerys had always thought it peculiar, though, that the scavengers didn't try to rob them as they left. In fact no one ever came near them on the return. They had been through as much as anyone could endure, now they were given safe passage. Or maybe it was because they both reeked of the monsters that had used them. They were feared because of their association.

As they reached the outskirts of the town, both of them felt a return to peak fitness, but mentally, they were shattered.

'I can't do this again,' said Mai.

'You can and you will,' Kerys said.

'How can you be so brave? How can you bear it?' Mai said.

Kerys knew the hinges of Mai's mind were at breaking point. Her own was teetering on the brink of insanity. It would be a blessing when they both finally snapped.

'We didn't burst,' laughed Mai realising belatedly that she had survived. 'We spewed out their brats and we didn't burst ...'

Kerys looked at the food in the cart. It seemed meagre for the effort. But they would live another month. What other choice was there left to them? It was live or die, the Old Ones ruled, darkness consumed the light, their offspring brats forced a new breed from the bellies of any remaining women willing to sell their souls.

*Death might be a better alternative,* Kerys thought. Others had taken that road.

'We're already in hell, nothing could be worse on the other side,' Mai said.

Kerys barely noticed that her friend often spoke aloud her own thoughts.

The docklands were a fair distance from the town, but they reached them just before full darkness came down. The potion was starting to wear off, and Mai's energy was failing. Kerys took over pushing the cart herself.

They arrived at their hovel to see the door wide open.

Kerys pushed the cart inside, then closed and locked the door. The former warehouse was full of dust and filth brought inside by the wind coming in from the sea.

Mai was on the brink of collapse now and Kerys set her down on the floor beside the cart.

'I'll check on the others,' Kerys said.

She hurried away. Inside the former offices Kerys found the children. They were all sitting nicely around the table, just as they had left them.

'Food is here,' Kerys said.

The children didn't reply. They waited as Kerys went away again and returned with Mai, who had recovered her breath, and the cart full of food.

Kerys helped Mai to a chair. She opened one of the cans which contained some kind of meat. Then she spooned it onto Mai's plate.

'You have to eat,' Kerys said.

Mai glanced around at the children. They all stared at her with glassy eyes. Then she began to eat her food. It was all for their sake after all.

Kerys went from one to the other, feeding them scraps of food.

'They are always so quiet,' Mai said. 'It's just not normal.'

Two more children had joined the group in their absence.

*I hope the food will last,* Kerys thought.

Then she sat down and lifted her tee-shirt. One of the new arrivals latched on, its long black appendages wrapped around her, pulsing like a boa constrictor. Mai squirmed as the second newborn crawled towards her, its slimy arms clawing at her chest. But she too lifted her top and let the monstrosity suckle.

After that the other children took their turn, though some now ate scraps of protein from their plates.

Kerys sang a lullaby as she nursed the last one. She placed a small kiss on the creature's cheek. The flesh was soft and squishy, its head like the bulbous body of an octopus. Bottomless black eyes stared back at her from an expressionless face that vaguely resembled a small child. Kerys smiled. A mother's love was a strange thing indeed.

She looked up at Mai and saw the other woman staring at her as though she were insane.

'We are never going to be free are we?' Mai said.

'Why would you want to be?' Kerys answered, the smile

back on her face as she rocked the child in her arms.

She had been to breaking point and beyond.

# Amatu

The *Nautilus* slid through the water like a scimitar blade, parting the waves as Captain Nemo steered

The vessel was stunning to behold inside and out, no luxury spared. It offered a lifestyle away from land that was sustainable and welcome to the men Nemo had recruited as crew. They were oddments of men. Some criminals, who, finding a new religion in Nemo, had signed over their lives to their guru. Nemo had no intention of abusing their trust. Merely a desire to lead them away from their former corruptions.

'To adventures, lads!' he said now, adopting an ironic piratical tone to which his loyal crew cheered. Every day was an adventure for them all, this wild journey through the sea to lands unseen by landlubber eyes.

Once out to sea, four large tanks - two front, two back - were opened up and sea water was sucked in. The vessel sank down slowly, controlled by Nemo as he steered it through the water. They were deep enough to glide under any oncoming ships unobserved, but not so deep that they would suffer ill effects. Though Nemo had taken precautions for this. There would be times when their explorations led them deeper into the sea and then, Nemo's secret weapon would be employed. He did not want his men to suffer the bends.

The crew didn't know that Nemo was on yet another personal mission.

They had landed in the Americas for a few weeks. Taking on fresh supplies before returning to the sea. By then Nemo and his men were itching to be beneath the waves, reminded as they were of how most landers thought of nothing more than their greed. Nemo paid over the odds for their supplies - coin meant nothing more to him than a means to gain what he needed.

The vessel pitched sideways and the metal construct groaned

as it adjusted to the pressure. There was a moment of tension as they moved deeper in the water. On the first voyage the crew had held their breath at this moment: was their genius leader right – could the *Nautilus* hold the ocean as bay? And then there was a shift of energy inside the vessel and they had known that they were safe. Though Nemo himself never doubted it.

As they went deeper, the pace had picked up and the crew felt the glorious speed of their ship as it raced under the water, scattering shoals of fish as it cut through the ocean. It was clear to everyone that Captain Nemo owned the sea.

They came above the surface just outside a small island somewhere in the South Pacific. This was mainly unchartered territory, but Nemo seemed to know exactly where he was going.

'Bring the chest,' Nemo ordered, and two of his crew, already primed, went to fetch a large wooden chest from Nemo's quarters.

Nemo didn't tell them what was inside, nor why they were here. It was one of the mysteries that the crew had to contend with. He never explained. But it was noted that when they were on land, a message had arrived for the captain that he had read over and over. The chest followed. It was taken onboard and stowed in the captain's quarters. Strict instructions followed that no one should attempt to open it. On pain of death.

There were a few curious souls among the crew, but none stupid enough to disobey a direct order.

The bulky trunk was loaded onto a small boat in the loading bay, and then the back of the *Nautilus* opened. With Nemo and six crew men aboard, the boat was launched into the water.

'Where are we?' asked one of the younger crew members.

'The natives call this place *Amatu*,' said Nemo by way of explanation. 'You will not find it on any map.'

The beach of *Amatu* approached as the small boat slid through the water with the same ease as the *Nautilus* had traversed the sea.

As they landed on the beach Nemo saw the Amatuan men

gathering on the sand. Then the men parted and another male came forward, taller than the rest, wearing an ornate head dress.

'Who are they?' asked one of the sailors.

'This is their holy man, a shaman of sorts. Do as I do,' Nemo said and he bowed down low before the man.

Nemo's men copied their captain, only standing back up once Nemo did. They were amazed that Nemo knew what to do, or how he understood the Amatuan shaman as he spoke to him.

'Bring the chest,' Nemo said. 'Carry it carefully for it contains a very precious cargo.'

Two of his men hurried to obey.

Then the small party passed by the other Amatuans as Nemo followed the shaman away from the beach.

The journey across the island was arduous and Nemo regularly swapped the men carrying the heavy chest, even taking a turn himself. They passed from beach to forest and then traversed more mountainous land until they reached the centre of the island.

A volcano lay at the island's heart. And chipped into the front of old cooled lava rock were some steps. Nemo changed the crew carrying the chest once more and now the original two men took over again.

'We must carry this to the top,' Nemo said. 'Take care for the steps are treacherous.'

He then instructed two more of his men to follow close behind the first two.

'Keep them steady,' he said to the second team. 'Be ready to support if one slips.'

The remaining two were to stay at the bottom. 'Face away from the volcano. Don't look back until I return,' Nemo told them.

Then Nemo went ahead, following the shaman as he led the way up the steps. He glanced over his shoulder to see that his men where behind and observed that both male and female Amatuans were now gathered at the volcano's foot.

The way up was as treacherous as Nemo had warned and the men carrying the chest slipped a couple of times, but each time they were supported by the other crew members below. It was a relief for them all when they reached the summit.

The top of the volcano was a flat ridge, forged over time by short bursts of eruptions. The two crewmen placed the chest down carefully at the foot of the shaman and then, taking Nemo's lead all of the *Nautilus* men bowed again.

'Whatever happens,' Nemo said, 'do not look at what is in the chest.'

In front of them the shaman tied a piece of cloth around his own eyes, and he yelled instructions down to the waiting Amatuans. Nemo observed that all of them turned away from the volcano and covered their eyes with their hands. There were no children among them and Nemo now saw the extent of the problem on the island. Infertility was rife and they would die out soon but for the drastic measure that had been taken. It was why he'd been called here, and why the thing inside the chest was so important to these people.

It had been stolen long ago by some foolish mortals who'd paid for their crime. The creature had been stored, kept from the eyes of men in the safety of a monastery, now, with the aid of Nemo's network the thing could be returned to its rightful home. The Amatuans would regain their ability to reproduce. There was an equilibrium that had to be maintained. Nemo saw it as his job to ensure this happened.

Nemo closed his eyes and bowed his head low. It was crucial that he did not look at the creature in the chest. He heard the shaman open it and then felt the shuddering touch of a tentacled appendage as it brushed across his head. Nemo didn't move, he knew what would happen if he looked up at the creature. Covering his head with his arms to avoid the temptation of looking, he waited for the creature to be drawn to the volcano flame below.

Then, Nemo heard a distinct and dreadful cry and he knew, that despite his warning one of his crew had been unable to resist looking at the creature.

The monster, having gained one victim, would have others, and so it touched and poked at all the men, hoping for the response of another.

'Don't look at it!' cried Nemo. 'Your very life depends on it!' but his warning fell on deaf ears as one by one each of his men opened their eyes to see the hideous creature that tormented them.

At last Nemo heard the creature descend. Only then did he open his eyes, but keeping them downcast as a precaution he backed away from the edge to the steps.

'It's gone,' said the shaman in Amatuan. 'And now our fertility ritual must begin.'

Nemo looked up then and saw the shaman's eyes were uncovered. His four men lay paralysed and mummified on the edge of the volcano.

He crawled to them. Their skin was parchment-thin but Nemo knew that every one of them still lived, trapped for eternity inside their own desiccated body.

'I have to relieve their suffering,' Nemo said.

'But how?' asked the shaman.

'I'm sorry,' he said to each of his men and then he took a sharp dagger from the holster on his belt and stabbed it firmly into the front of each of the men's foreheads. Stabbing so hard that he destroyed their brains as painlessly and efficiently as he could.

'We will give them an honourable burial,' the shaman said. He gave the order for some of his men to come and take away the bodies.

Nemo followed as the men were lifted down. He was saddened by the needless sacrifice and would have to explain to the remaining crew what had happened.

It was a tough lesson that they would all learn from though. For as their voyages continued there was every likelihood that they would deal once more with the Great Old Ones, some worse than Ghatanothoa, who resided once more in the Amatuan volcano.

Nemo left the island in the small boat and headed back to the *Nautilus*. Once on board he gave orders to depart the island and they soon submerged. It was unlikely that he would come this way again, but he knew now, despite the sacrifices that had been made, that the people of Amatu would live on.

# Keeping the Faith

It had been one of those rare wet summer nights. The air felt fresher for it, but Dominique could smell the dampness of the leaves and the rain had soaked into the dry dusky earth, turning it rapidly to mud. Her feet slipped as she trundled along the path through the woods. She always felt safe passing through here at night, but never dared to do it during the day. That was when the haters usually marked you. This was always a concern, even though she had done nothing wrong and should have nothing to fear.

The KKK hadn't struck in Biloxi for a few months. That was because no blacks had dared raise their heads. Not since April 4, 1968 when Martin Luther King was shot dead. They were all downtrodden here now - just as the white-folks wanted them.

Dominique slipped quietly through the trees. The walk from the big house, where she served as cook, cleaner and child-minder, was over two miles, but she was used to the exercise. It kept her lean, unlike some of her friends who took the bus back from the neighbourhoods where they worked. They all enjoyed eating the good food they prepared for their white employees too much. But Dominique never ate in a white woman's kitchen. It was against her religion to eat anywhere but in her own home, from her own plates, and the food she grew herself, along with the animals she personally caught and killed. Though this was rare, and so she ate mostly vegetables taken from the sanctified earth in her garden.

She saw a rabbit poke its nose out of a small hole. The animal sniffed the air, but didn't recognize Dominique as a threat until she had it caught in around the neck with a wire lasso. She pulled it up out of the hole. The animal wriggled and tugged, feet kicking as though it could still hop away, but the lasso tightened with every struggle slowly choking it to death. When the deed was done, Dominique pulled her paring knife free of the big purse she carried. She skinned the animal, then wrapped the remains up in the thick cloth she carried in her bag for this purpose. She could eat well for a few days now. Rabbit stew might even last for a week.

At that moment Dominique heard a sound. She hid silently behind the broad beam of an old oak and waited until the man passed. She couldn't see who he was, or tell if he were black or white in the dark, as he was wearing a thick overcoat, and a hat pulled down over his eyes to ward of the final dribbles of rain. Dominique remained hidden until he was long gone and she could no longer hear the sound of his clothing brushing against the bushes and trees. Then she hurried home with her prize. It wouldn't have been good for her to be found with the rabbit. Not on this land.

Back home the rite of eating began. She prepared the rabbit. Seared its flesh in oil before plunging the cut up meat into a huge stewing pot. Then she added fresh carrots, sweet potato, and green beans, all taken fresh from her garden that morning. After that she said her ritual words: words she had heard all of her life. The thing the minister called 'Speaking in tongues'. Dominique had them burned into her brain after years of watching her mother cook.

She slept while the stew boiled, waking instinctively a few hours later when the meat was tender and cooked. Then she scooped a small portion up into a bowl and she sat by the electric fire eating slowly, mopping up the final dregs with homemade bread. Afterwards Dominique slept again.

'Girl, you gotta get some meat on those bones,' said Clara the next morning as Dominique left her small house. 'You is looking skinny as a skellington.'

She knew that Clara thought she was odd. That the whole of the community wondered at her stubborn refusal to marry one of the local church-going men. But Dominique liked being alone. She couldn't imagine sharing her time with anyone else, especially when she had to spend so much of it with her employers and their children.

She nodded to Clara. 'I eat. I just don' like white-folks' food is all ... you look like you eat way too much of it.'

Clara laughed. She was always happy and hard to insult but Dominique's behaviour since the day King died confused her. It *frightened* her in a way she couldn't define. No amount of good nature good shake that feeling.

'What is it with you,' she'd asked a few days after the assassination when she saw the weight dropping from Dominique. 'We's all upset, girl. But you can't make yo'self sick over it. That way they all won. We jus' gotta lay low for awhile ...'

'This ain't about King,' Dominique said. 'I'm following the religion my Momma always talked about.'

Clara had looked at Dominique cynically. 'Yo' momma was crazy to th' end. Yo' don' wanna go that way.'

Dominique said nothing. She knew her mother hadn't been insane but she couldn't explain things to Clara without exposing herself and her faith to the scrutiny of her friend. It was unwise to say anything more although she knew Clara meant well. Clara was still nevertheless devoutly Christian: the white man's faith that had been forced on their ancestors and yet, they had all taken to it. Dominique didn't believe it though. What god would care if your skin was black, white or something in-between? She saw the church as something the white-folks also had control of. She questioned the way that salvation only seemed to be for those it deemed worthy. But it was also for precisely this reason that Dominique continued to go to church on Sundays. Although she mostly tuned out the minister and his bible bashing rants she didn't want anyone to notice her by her absence. She enjoyed the singing though, and always took part in this with enthusiasm.

Clara climbed on the bus. 'Yo' comin'?'

The vile smell of sweat, wafted from the open door. Dominique hesitated, as she always did, but she knew she had no choice but to be cooped up inside this bus for the short distance. Even though it didn't take long, the feeling of it suffocated her but she couldn't risk her walk through the forest in the daytime, and so she had no real choice.

She stepped on. She was carrying a basket with a pie and some candied apples for the little ones in her care. The apples were taken from the tree in her garden and so were blessed, as was the content of the pie. Dominique liked to take the children these treats. She hoped the pure food would stave off the meanness that their parents had inside them.

She sat down next to Clara, who noticed the frown as Dominique glanced down at the stained seat.

'Yo' need to get over them airs and graces, girl, or yo' is gonna get yo'self in a whole heap o' trouble. And I ain't talking about the ...' Clara looked around then lowered her voice to a whisper, '... KKK.'

Dominique said nothing - she knew how it went with the church types. They could excommunicate her and then she would be out on a limb, left exposed to the likes of those who felt like beating on a black for the fun of it. There was no real law enforcement in the town, not when it came to crimes committed to blacks, even though the white officers pretended to investigate. The fact was if a death occurred to a white, the town was turned upside down, and someone, guilty or not, was always blamed and tried for the crime. But, if it was a black that was killed or injured then no such thing ever happened.

The journey seemed interminable but Dominique tried to think of other things until finally her stop approached and she climbed off the bus. She walked up the huge driveway to Mayor Jackson's house. Then skirted around the back to the kitchen entrance. Once inside, Dominique stowed her bag, hung up her coat, and smoothed her hands down her maid's uniform. After placing the pie in the larder she headed off to the nursery.

'Dominique! Thank goodness you're here.'

'Is everythin' alright Miss Ellie?'

'Marcus has been up all night with a cough. It sounds like a barking dog. I've been so frightened and I'm so tired,' Miss Ellie said.

She looked so frail and weak that Dominique feared she was going to drop the baby.

'Don't yo' worry none. I'll take him,' Dominique said holding out her hands.

At that moment Marcus burst into a round of coughing.

'Tha's croup, Miss Ellie. I needs to take him into the bathroom.'

'Why? What you gonna do?'

'I knows the best cure for this. He be fine. I promise.'

Dominique took Marcus into the bathroom and began to run hot water into the bath. The room rapidly filled with steam, and as the child breathed in the moist air the coughing fit slowly diminished. By the time she returned the baby to the nursery, Miss Ellie was back in her bedroom and fast asleep.

After that the day was fairly routine and Dominique continued with her chores while keeping an eye on Marcus, even though she knew that the worst of the croup had passed.

She left later than usual, making sure that the baby was warm and settled.

'He be fine now, Miss Ellie,' she reassured. 'But if he start again, yo' just run the hot water in the bathroom like I tol' yo'.'

'Can't I persuade you to stay over? We can put somethin' down on the nursery floor for you to sleep ...'

'Not tonight. But I promise he gon' be fine.'

Miss Ellie let her leave reluctantly, but Dominique had no intention of staying all night no matter how worried the woman was. She needed to get back, perform her ritual and tonight, after all, was a sacred night in her mother's faith.

After the rite of eating, Dominique slipped back outside. The small ghetto where she and the other blacks lived had no street lighting. It was to her advantage though the others complained about how difficult it was when they returned home late. She passed by Clara's house, all was silent in there. Probably because, Billy, Clara's drunk of a husband, hadn't yet returned from his nightly visit to the bar downtown. Dominique barely thought about Clara's troubles though, tonight she had enough to think about. Tonight was the night she had been preparing for since April, 4$^{th}$, almost three months ago. In the Christian calendar there was nothing special about this night. It was, however, a very special night when it came to the ancient faith. The one that her people had all but forgotten. Not her mother though, she had been chosen to carry the mantel all of her life, and just before her passing she had imparted the knowledge on her daughter.

Cleansed by the months of denying herself the taste of contaminated food, cleansed by her prayers and rituals, Dominique was ready to present herself to the god. It was time.

She slipped into the woodland as a group of white teenagers drove through the ghetto in a battered truck. They were drunk and looking for trouble and this was the place they would find it. Dominique stared out of the brush unseen as the truck pulled up in front of the preacher's house. *So, they are attacking the Reverend now?* But all the boys did was throw empty beer bottles at the road sign. Then, quickly growing bored, they climbed back into the truck and drove away.

Dominique let out the breath she had been holding. If they had attacked the preacher, that would have meant serious problems erupting at a crucial time. It was something she didn't want right now. Something she had to avoid at all costs.

The trees swallowed her. She found her way easily to the ritual site. It was where the KKK had done most of their burnings, never knowing how they were fouling a sacred area, but of course this was all to Dominique's advantage. The God would be willing to listen to her more now. He had no love for anything that did not worship him, regardless of colour of skin. And that burning cross was an affront to him, not a tribute.

The clearing was empty as she approached. Even in the dark Dominique could see the scorched earth that marred the once perfect meadow.

Dominique knelt in the ashes.

The last local man to disappear was Freddy Johnson. Dominique had gone to school with Freddy. He had been a good man, a god-fearing church-goer that had been sweet on her once. His wife and children suffered his loss now, while the local sheriff implied Freddy must have run off with another woman. It wasn't his way. Dominique knew that.

She touched the ash, then brought it to her lips. She tasted it. Freddy's face flashed before her eyes.

*'String this nigger up, boys,' said the tallest man in the group.*

*A group of men stood in a circle around their makeshift crucifix, as Freddy was tied in a parody of Jesus, arms outstretched, legs crossed at the ankle. Blood poured from his nose like paint splashed on a wall. His nose was busted, would probably never be straight again, and his eyes were swollen to small slits.*

*The men were dressed in white robes, tall pointed headdresses covered their faces, leaving only the barest gaps for their mean eyes to gaze out at their victim.*

*Freddy struggled as a burning torch was touched to a pile of dry wood beneath his feet. The kindling soon caught, the dry foliage burst into flame and the men in the white robes backed away for fear of being sucked into the blaze. Freddy screamed as the first heat burst over his legs and flames licked like orange tongues up his ankles, over his thighs and lit up his dirt and blood stained clothing. He vented his bowels. Then the screaming stopped and mercifully Freddy blacked out with pain and shock.*

*The white robed men stood like featureless statues around the body until it burnt and only moved again hours later, when the body, wood crucifix and all evidence was nothing more than ashes.*

The vision ended and Dominique came back to the reality of her surroundings. The forest was quiet. She glanced up above and saw the full moon lighting the clearing and felt its cold flame lick across her dark, plaited head. The time was approaching and panic briefly swelled inside her as she began to doubt, felt the fear that if she was wrong, if her mother had been insane ... but no! Dominique knew the truth. The God lay here, ancient and timeless, strong and powerful, he would smite the bad for all of their cruel meaningless deeds. This was truly a god that cared about its followers.

'Tuatha m'were men,' Dominique said as she stood. 'In f'aray. B'in casai.'

The words of ritual poured from her lips like molten lava and pain echoed in the recesses of every thin and tender limb as she was tested.

'Adnoai, carimenai.'

The blood in her veins burned but still she spoke the language of the god, telling him that she was her servant.

Dominique did not call for justice in her prayers, nor did she beg for blessings from the god. All she wished for was to wake him. Let him see what the world had now become. As dawn filtered through the sky, she fell prostrate and exhausted at the foot of the ancient tree.

Nothing stirred as she dragged her tired body back to the ghetto and fell down onto her bed. Then she allowed sleep to take her.

It was Sunday and her day off from the big house, even so, Dominique pulled herself up from the bed and prepared for the church service. If she hurried she would just make it. She heard the church bell ring as she pulled on her clothes, then she glanced out into the street. What she saw outside struck real terror in her heart. Ten men, all dressed in long white robes, wearing pointed white headdresses, stood at her garden gate. She tried to see into the eye slits as they stared at her kitchen window. Then one by one, they turned, climbed into an open top jeep and drove away.

After that Dominique was too afraid to leave the house.

'Dominique,' said Clara as she banged loudly on her door, 'Is yo' okay?'

Dominique struggled to the door. She felt old, weary. Her bones ached but she opened the door, then backed up to allow Clara entrance.

'I is sick,' she said and it wasn't a lie.

'Yo' look bad, girl. What I tol' you about eating right?'

'I be fine. It's just tiredness is all. I needs to rest. They bin working me bad at the house.'

'Yeah. That Miss Ellie don' know much about housekeeping so's I heard,' Clara said. 'Ain't much on the mothering side either.'

'She okay,' Dominique said generously. 'But her husband, the judge, he ain't home much.'

'I'll make you some soup,' Clara suggested.

'I has some. I be fine. You take care now and I see you in the mornin' after I git some sleep.'

Clara left reluctantly and Dominique switched on the cooker and began to warm her rabbit stew, but as she turned the wooden spoon around the bowl she realized the stew had spoilt. She tipped it away, took fresh vegetables from the garden and began to prepare them. However every carrot she scraped dissolved in her hands as though they had been picked weeks ago and left to rot.

'Somethin' wrong,' Dominique said allowed. 'Somethin' very wrong. My garden is spoilt. Ain't sacred no more ...'

She looked out of the window and saw the once perfect lines of fresh food now full of weeds.

'What I done?'

She thought back to the night before and the intense ritual. Her mother had told her so carefully. She was sure she hadn't done things wrong, but why? Why had the KKK been outside her house like they knew what she had done? Why was her pure garden now spoilt? Why did she feel so sick inside, like somehow the devil had gotten inside her and was rotting her too, just like the fruit on the apple tree?

It felt like the longest day but as night drew in Dominique's strength returned. It was still a full moon out and she knew that she had to go back to the clearing and straighten out what she had done wrong. The god would be waiting for her return. She had asked for nothing, just as her mother insisted she must do. Yet she felt she had entered into a bargain of sorts, something that required payment.

With renewed vigour Dominique hurried through the trees and back to the clearing but as she approached a new fear began to wheedle its way into her mind. She felt cold, despite the intense heat and she constantly thought about the KKK standing outside of her home as though they knew she had done something wrong.

The clearing was empty and something had changed. For a moment Dominique couldn't put her finger on what was different and then she realised. The tree. The ancient Oak. It was *gone.*

She prostrated herself once more at the site where it had stood. Now a gaping hole remained, as though the hand of god had ripped the tree from the ground, roots and all.

'Ilya 'em mai. Tuatha m'were men. In f'aray. B'in casai.'

A roar of pure hatred echoed through the clearing.

'You see!' said a voice behind her. 'She's some kinda witch.'

Dominique turned to find the thing she most feared. Ten men, all members of the KKK wearing their full disguise. Though inexplicably she knew every one of them. The robes hid nothing from her eyes. She felt renewed. Strong. Part of nature in a way that she had never experienced despite her love of all things natural.

There was the judge - now she knew why his wife was always home alone at night. The Sheriff and some of his men lurked amongst them. The doctor was there and Dominique recalled the day she helped him to deliver the judge's son, Marcus. The white preacher's eldest son. She knew them all! Had dealt with them one way or another.

'I'm no witch,' Dominique said but she knew they wouldn't believe her. They would burn her now, just like Freddy and all those other people whose ashes scattered the clearing.

'What did you do to that tree?' the judge asked.

'Me? I didn't do nothin' Judge. I just come here and it be gone.'

The judge took a sharp breath in.

'You know me?' he asked.

'I knows you all. Yo's gonna have to kill me now I reckon.'

The preacher's son began to panic. Dominique remembered his name then. Ethan. She had never liked him. His eyes had always been strange, like he was looking her over as if he could see through her clothing.

'How does she know us?' Ethan murmured.

'Hush now, it's just guessing. You know how they like to try and guess,' said the doctor.

'Yes Doc Bailey, I reckon all us niggers try to guess whose killin' them. Bet that was jus' on poor Freddy's mind when you set that torch at his feet.'

'Hush your mouth!' said the judge. 'You're signing your own death warrant.'

'We ain't killed a woman before,' Ethan said. His voice betrayed the excitement the thought gave him. Dominique felt that cold chill seeping further into her bones. Now though, the fear had left her. She felt different. Strong. Invincible. As though the words of prayer to the god had enforced her with some form of supernatural inner strength.

*Perhaps this is how it be when you face death,* she thought. *Once you knows it's comin' you don't fear it no more.*

'What's up with her eyes?' Ethan said. 'Let's kill this crazy bitch, but let's have some fun with her first.'

They descended on her, not caring now that the awkward pointed hats came askew, that she could see all of their faces for real, because they were definite in their decision to kill her. There was a mad frenzy, a tearing at her clothing. Dominique didn't struggle. They stretched her out naked on the spot where the shadow from the huge tree once fell, and as the judge dropped his pants and kneeled between her legs ready to do what he'd always wanted to do to the young, slender maid that cleaned his house, something peculiar occurred. Dominique could see inside him. See all the hatred and lust and sickness that drove the man to kill. Each of these men didn't have a particular hatred for blacks, they hated anything that was different from them. Bigotry and stupidity was their excuse to do something that their dark souls craved. They killed. They justified the murders because they saw the victims as less than themselves.

'Jezus! What's happening?'

The judge fell back from her suddenly. Dominique felt no pain but she could see the transformation in their minds. They saw the growing limbs, branch-like, as hideous.

She was standing again. Tall and proud, towering over them as she grew. Ethan tried to run, but her long arm swept the air, connected with his head and the loud crack as his neck snapped with the hard blow gave Dominique a feeling of satisfaction. His death energy fuelled another growth spurt. The doctor backed away, almost to the edge of the clearing, Dominique tried to follow, but it was difficult to move her legs as roots sprang from her feet and buried themselves deeper and deeper in the ground. But her arms, no her branches, stretched out and reached him. She swoop him up, throwing him into the air. Some short distance away, the doctors body crashed back down and he lay screaming as his shattered spine destroyed the use of his legs. Dominique knew the damage was permanent.

Then there was the judge - he struggled to straighten his pants and Dominique caught him as he stumbled away. Her fingers were small branches now, but no less easy to manipulate.

'I knowed what was in your mind judge. I knowed it all along. You aint gonna father no more children ...' she said. Her voice was big, as big as her body was, and Dominique marvelled at how her words sounded, even to herself, like thunder that could talk.

Her long fingers turned sharp and she pierced the judge's scrotum, ripping back in a crude attempt at castration. The judge screamed. Dominique smiled, but her face barely moved. She placed the judge down, then turned to finish the rest of the KKK members. It didn't take long to give each of them what they deserved.

As the blood and carnage filled the clearing, the red fluid poured into the empty hole and Dominique's roots sucked the life's liquid into her truck. She felt nourished, pure and her legs took one final step back to fill the gap. She stretched her arms up towards the heavens, even as she felt the essence of the ancient god, a red mist spirit, merge with her force.

Then she knew. Only the pure could join with the god. Only the cleansed. Only those with true faith.

She felt her roots settle and the huge trunk shuddered a final time. She had asked for nothing but had been given the greatest gift of all.

# Sacrifice

Captain Nemo stared out, unblinking, into the dark blue depths and let his mind wander into the realms of creativity that could only be found below the surface. Deep in the ocean, in his own giant isolation tank, the world above, and the concerns of man, couldn't touch him. His pupils were dilated. He had not surfaced for more than a year and although this did not alarm him, sometimes his crew needed to see land; walk on soil; take respite with a whore or two.

The time to resurface was rapidly approaching.

He let his mind float, barely registering the sea life that swam before the expansive window, as he turned the *Nautilus* slowly around. He was only half aware of the navigation system bleeping agreement that he was turning in the right direction and the slight upsurge of whirring as the engine boosters kicked in. Nemo needed no guidance. He knew the ocean like the palm of his own hand. The technology was for his pilot, not for himself: he could not be at the helm for all hours of the day.

Nemo was the son of an Indian raja, and his olive skin would have been darker but for the fact that the captain rarely saw daylight. From an early age he had been raised in England, brought up as a man of privilege and wealth. As a result Nemo spoke in a cultured English voice. He had been educated to a high standard, soon surpassing his tutors, and mostly dressed as any English gentleman might. However, at sea he wore a beard which gave him a distinct pirate air.

The *Nautilus* shuddered. Nemo blinked, bringing his focus back from the water to the submarine around him. Sometimes he forgot completely that there was anything but himself and the sea.

The earth trembled and the *Nautilus* shook so badly

Nemo thought it might judder completely apart leaving himself and the crew out in the middle of the ocean. He gripped the wheel as violent jerking rocked the submarine threatening to turn it on its head.

Nemo turned the vessel into the flow of the water in order to regain control. His efforts kept the *Nautilus* upright. Then, aftershocks rippled through the water. He almost lost control of the wheel but held on with more determination than physical strength.

A few moments later the sea around the vessel began to calm and the sickly rocking motion subsided as the craft regained its equilibrium. Only then did Nemo hear the red alert bell that was ringing all over the submarine.

He straightened up slackening his grip on the wheel, then pushed one hand back through his untidy hair.

'Captain?' said a voice.

Nemo turned his head to look at the man who sat to his left on the bridge beside a complicated station. A panel of buttons, an echo-location screen, and several flashing lights illuminated the area, while the red lights, flickering on and off, reflected in the crewman's eyes.

The crew member was André: one of the youngest in his mid-twenties. He hadn't been travelling with them for more than two years, but André had been a lost soul, and Nemo had taken him in, training the man's keen mind. André, Nemo knew, would be his finest engineer one day. But he was still young and had not yet fully given himself to the life at sea that the others had. It took time, after all, to eradicate the damage parents did to their young on land. Only the sea's calming influence could take away all of the hurt.

'The monitors are showing serious disruption ahead,' said André unaware of Nemo's thoughts about him. 'We should turnabout ...'

'We've fielded earthquakes before,' Nemo said.

'This looks ...'

At a sign from the captain the pilot stepped in and took the helm and Nemo moved to André's side. He studied the instruments, understanding far more than anyone else could have.

'... more serious than you realise,' Nemo said finishing the sentence that André failed to find words for. The earthquake was coming from Europe.

Returning to the helm, Nemo typed in several complex coordinates into the navigation system. They would navigate around the disruption, but end up near the source of the problem. Then Nemo would be able to assess the level of damage and its continued effect on the sea.

'Notify me when we are 20 miles from destination,' he told the pilot. The man nodded, never taking his eyes from the glass window in front of him.

Nemo left the deck, his mind no longer floating in the depths of the sea, but fully focused on the interior of the *Nautilus* and the possible damage that the earthquake had done to his ship.

They surfaced at dawn, and as the water cleared the top balcony, a portal opened and Nemo and several of his crew emerged. Nemo breathed in the air and found it unclean. Ahead they saw a port flooded by the sea, its natural bank destroyed. Beach front property ruined. The air and land smelt scorched. Brick and mortar appeared to have been melted by some form of intense heat.

'Marseille?' said André.

Nemo's silence confirmed the young man's fears: his former home, normally a bustling international shipping port was destroyed, but by what?

Nemo looked over the destroyed port before returning below. They submerged again and the crew waited for instruction as the submarine sank.

Nemo looked through the large window once more but his mind was elsewhere. He was remembering a promise he had once made.

'To England,' Nemo said.

A large panel opened in the side of the *Nautilus*, and a launch ramp slowly slid out and sloped down towards the water. A few moments later a small boat glided onto the calm water. Throughout the short journey Nemo had been monitoring the earth tremors, and there was definite activity coming from London.

At the helm, Nemo turned the small boat into the natural current. They entered the mouth of the Thames at London's Docklands and then, Nemo fired the engine. The ship was powered by steam, and a crew member in the small engine room below, fed sea-based dried plant life into the furnace to keep the heat pumping to the water heater. Steam pushed through the engine, moving the rudders underneath the boat, while smoke poured out from a funnel that passed through the deck and towered above the helm.

As he passed down the Thames, Nemo saw the toppled tower, sans its huge clock face, half spilt into the water. The parliament houses had fared no better. The walls were punctured with holes, windows smashed, and the roof appeared to have crumpled into the building itself.

'What caused this?' asked André.

For once Nemo was lost for an explanation. Even so, he attempted to rationalise the destruction.

'War perhaps …'

'Between the French and English?' André said.

'No. Neither country has the science to do this … It's too … complete. Too devastating.'

Nemo recalled his youth as he studied the crumbled building. It occurred to him that the enemy had somehow managed to achieve what Guy Fawkes never could: the total downfall of the country and its leadership.

His mind went then to the Queen.

*'Protect my seas and you will always have a home on England's shores …' Victoria had said.*

*'Always …' Nemo had promised.*

'It has to be some form of invasion,' Nemo said. His guilt at failing England was a rock in his gut. But how was he to know this would happen?

André had barely left his side since the first discovery of the anomaly that had affected the *Nautilus*.

'Invasion?' Andre said.

Nemo looked upwards. It had to have come from the stars.

Nemo pulled the small boat into a dock - little more than steps that led up from the Thames to the ruined Houses of Parliament - and then, Andre jumped to the small barely damaged pier and secured the ropes. Two other crew men joined him and the boat was tied down as Nemo turned off the engine.

The smell of steam had been masking the burnt odour that permeated the air.

'Remain with the boat,' Nemo said.

The engineer who had been feeding the engine below now took up post by the helm as ordered as Nemo climbed out and led the other crewmen up the steps.

They walked through the ruins. Burnt leather chairs, bodies charred to the bone, and the inner workings of Big Ben, lay at their feet. The air smelt like cooked meat and the men were forced to cover their noses to prevent themselves gagging.

Nemo ignored the smell but frowned as he made his way through the remains. The ground beneath his feet was hot. Smoke billowed up from the ruins. The heat in the air burnt his skin, singed his eyebrows and beard.

Then he saw it: a towering monstrosity, stalking among the ruins like a scavenger picking at the remnants of the dead. It tottered impossibly on three legs, but had numerous tentacle-like appendages.

Could this thing be something to do with the old gods?

Nemo shrank back behind the remains of a support wall. This thing was machine, not animal, though possibly was operated by someone or thing. Nemo took a pair of binoculars out of his pocket and peered through them from his vantage point. Up close he could see a huge eye-like window - blood red - but not what was behind it. The beast of machinery moved away from Nemo, unaware that prey lay in such close proximity, and only when it was several hundred feet away did Nemo dare to expel the breath he was holding. He quelled the tremor in his hands as he lowered the binoculars. André saw it.

'What *was* that?' André said.

'Something not of this earth.'

The towering machine moved farther away and then, as though it had seen some movement, a blazing surge of heat poured from the red eye. The weapon repeated firing and white hot flame burst over one of the still standing structures. The building toppled.

'Some kind of heat ray,' Nemo said. 'I wonder how they have managed to create that?'

Remaining unseen wasn't too difficult for Nemo and his men as they followed the machine at a safe distance. About a half a mile away from the Thames Nemo saw the alien mechanism pause before the wreckage of an old tavern. Like lightning one of the metallic tentacles weaved outwards and scooped something up. They were close enough that they could see the creature raise a prone figure. It was a woman. The eye moved, the red shield blinked like the second eyelid of a reptile, and then a long needle-thin implement, held by one of the tentacle limbs, pressed sharply into the arm of the woman.

It was only then that she moved and Nemo realised she was still alive.

André jumped beside him, 'We have to do something ...'

'We cannot defeat this thing. Nothing can ' Nemo said.

The woman woke then and screamed, squirming against the obvious invasion until her voice broke and her body lapsed into shock. When the alien had retracted all that it wanted, it callously tossed the body aside, throwing it roughly back into the debris.

The woman now lay, eyes wide open, body broken. She was, Nemo surmised, dead before she had hit the ground.

The machine moved in its peculiar jerky fashion and now,

much to the horror of Nemo's crewmen, it fed the blood from its victim back into its own body.

'How horrible!' gasped André. 'Is there nothing that can be done?'

The *Nautilus* submerged, pulling out into open ocean moving as fast as possible from the shore and the wasteland that was once London.

No, there was nothing that could be done. England had fallen, now all that remained was the safe haven of open sea.

Nemo gave a set of coordinates to his pilot and then retired to his private quarters. Once alone he lay on his bed considering the dilemma that now faced him. He, Nemo, had no need of land. He would happily never resurface if it wasn't for the occasional luxury. They proved every day that the sea's harvest was enough to live on. They needed nothing they couldn't find under the ocean. What would happen when these creatures finished with their murder of man? Would they then go onto animal and sea life?

He could see this as a likely scenario. It meant he had to act. His honour was at stake. A promise made, even to a queen that was probably dead, was still something he had to see through. Even if it meant his own demise.

Nemo closed his eyes. He needed to sleep. To think.

He felt the pull of open sea around the exterior of the *Nautilus*. He wondered if any of his men were aware of these subtle ripples. Now, he could even sense a change in the tide, an anti-flow to the water, as though it were pulling back from the shore in an attempt to avoid the monstrosities that now ruled the land.

Curious about this sensation, and sure of what he would find, Nemo pressed a button on a panel beside his bed. The side of his cabin opened and he could see out into the ocean through a clear glass window. He sat up. Outside there was a swarm of fish, all shapes and sizes, swimming in the same direction as the submarine - away from shore - and the *Nautilus* was passing through them.

'You know, don't you?' he said as if the fish could hear him.

The *Nautilus* was part of the shoal as it made its way at speed.

Nemo had always believed that fish were intelligent. They had stronger survival instincts than would at first be obvious and their deliberate behaviour now proved his theory. What else could explain this mass exodus? It was not the right season for migration, and anyway, not all of the sea life would migrate at the same time of year would they?

Nemo moved to the window and stood looking out. The fish swirled around the dense glass, flanking the vessel.

'You *know* ...' he said again. 'And I believe you may even be trying to tell me something.'

The idea formed then – perhaps the fish, behaving with such purpose, *were* communicating with him. He believed it, as certainly as he knew what he had to do next.

Some years ago, too many to recall, he had made a deal with the gods of the sea: the Deep Ones did not bother Nemo, and he did not encroach on any of their sacred realms. Though to Nemo, the entire ocean was sacred. There were, however, some places that the *Nautilus*'s ever circling route purposefully avoided.

The deal he had made had meant sacrifice, any further deals would require such again. Nemo wasn't sure that he could be so callous a second time, but then, what choice did he really have if it meant the salvation of the planet?

Nemo left his cabin and returned to the helm. The coordinates he had given the pilot would not do after all, but the place to which the *Nautilus* now needed to go was nowhere near the planned direction.

'Rest old friend,' Nemo said to the pilot. 'For you will be needed later on.'

The pilot nodded and left the bridge. Nemo took up the helm, but he did not program the new coordinates in the navigation system. This was a place that must only remain inside his head.

Twelve hours later Nemo had fallen into his usual trance state as he watched the water part for the *Nautilus*. The fish shoal was left far behind and the pilot returned.

'Captain, you need to trust me now and take rest yourself,' the pilot said.

Nemo stepped back and he whispered the coordinates for the change of course to the man.

'It's an island just 40 miles hence,' he explained. 'I'll be in my cabin but call me when you have it in sight.'

Sometime later Nemo woke to the whistling sound of his communicator. He leapt from his bed, agile and instantly awake. A few hours had passed and he was refreshed, despite the short time he had been able to sleep.

'Captain?' said the pilot as Nemo lifted the long thin tube and pressed it against his ear. 'We see the island. What would you like us to do?'

Nemo moved the tube to his mouth.

'Prepare the launch ...'

Once again the small craft launched into open water, this time a rowing boat was attached to the back and Nemo let André steer towards the island.

The deck was full of baskets of wine, cheeses, whiskeys and liqueurs, cured, smoked hams and sides of salmon. Beside them lay rolls of fabric. Fine silks from Asia, cotton from the Americas, and rolls of colourful ribbon from England.

'Take note,' Nemo said to the crew, and even those who were working to keep the boat moving gave the captain a measure of attention that assured him that they were listening. 'When we land you must bring these baskets of luxuries on shore. We have a very solemn task to do.'

No one questioned him, but the crew went unnaturally quiet while they worked. Even though Nemo had not expressed his motives, it was clear to them that he planned to *buy* something from the island natives. Since the *Nautilus* coffers were full to the brim with all manner of gold and jewels, the crew could only speculate on what that thing might be.

They weighed anchor and the rowing boat was pulled clear from the back. Relays began from the small boat to the pebbly shore. The baskets and fabric, as well as the men to carry them, were slowly conveyed onto the island.

By the time the final boatload reached the land, Nemo had prepared a convoy of men and they moved away from the shore, quickly subsumed into the tropical forest.

Nemo knew exactly where he was going. As the newest crew member André assumed that the men had been to this island before, but when Nemo paused to take stock of the landscape, the others floundered, often looking back over their shoulder in a vain attempt to see the shore. But Nemo's pauses were never for long and as he glanced at his pocket compass for a final time, the captain led his men with confident strides into the heart of the island.

They came out of the forest into a clearing. Ahead were primitive, ancient structures that spoke of a long lived society. Old buildings carved into the rock face surrounded one central tower. It was a mass of stone steps that climbed to a high platform.

'Whatever happens do not speak, or react,' Nemo said. 'Place the baskets at the bottom of the temple.'

André was the first to move towards the centre tower, and he placed his load down at the foot of the steps. As he backed away he glanced upwards and there he saw a robed figure, wearing an ornate feathered headdress. He was holding some type of long staff and appeared to be looking down on them. Despite his curiosity André did not linger and he moved away and stood behind Nemo waiting for further instruction. The other crewmen followed suit.

Warriors appeared as if from nowhere, and Nemo and his men were surrounded. The native arrivals carried spears, which they held ready to throw. The warriors wore their hair long, flowing over naked shoulders and one of them, who stepped forward as though he were their leader, had hair that reached almost to his ankles which was pulled up and away from his face but poured down his back. Each of them wore a loin cloth but little else, but their faces and torsos were scarred and marked with intricate drawings.

Nemo walked up to the temple steps and kneeled before them, his men did the same. They waited. Above their heads, the robed figure waved the staff as he drew invisible pictures in the air.

As the sun went down the robed figure descended from his tower. Then at the bottom he spoke to Nemo in a language that only the captain could understand.

'The day has come,' the priest said. 'I saw the signs in the sky.'

'Devils from another planet plague the world,' Nemo confirmed.

'Mars,' The priest said. 'They have always turned covetous eyes on earth.'

The priest raised his staff and all of the warriors surrounding the sailors backed away lowering their spears.

'We need a sacrifice. But your loss must be rewarded,' Nemo said he waved his hand at the offering beneath the temple.

The priest was quiet for a moment as though he were weighing up the validity of the offering.

'It must be someone of note for such a worthy task,' he said. Then he turned to the long haired warrior. 'Bring me the Chief's daughter.'

The girl did not struggle or make any attempt to escape as they led her back to the shore, onto the rowing boat and then, finally onto the small craft. She remained silent. The very image of dignity, yet surely she knew that something unpleasant was to befall her? She was young, perhaps no more than 18. She had shoulder length hair, unlike the warriors of her race, and wore a modest dress that covered her completely. She kept her large brown eyes lowered, and sat on the seat she was offered with her hands resting in her lap. There was no sign of distress or fear in her but her delicate jaw was set with serious determination.

'Take the lady to the guest cabin,' Nemo instructed André as they boarded the *Nautilus* André nodded but he had always thought it strange that they had a spare, 'guest' cabin, since there were never any guests, invited or otherwise, on the *Nautilus*. Nonetheless he took the girl to the room as instructed and although she did not appear to be able to speak their language she still understood that she must follow the young sailor and did so without reservation.

'You'll be safe in here,' said André.

The girl said nothing but went inside the big, plush room. André noted that clothing had been laid out for her on the bed, and a bathtub filled with hot water had been placed behind a modest screen. Also, there were two of the female crew waiting for the girl inside. These, André knew, were the *Nautilus* nursing staff, and he only ever saw them whenever a crewman became injured. He did not know where they even slept onboard, but suspected that they were on the top level near the medical facility. Few people actually had clearance to go up there and only when they were injured or sick were they ever permitted.

The guest suite was in the middle of the vessel, on the same level as the bridge and the captain's own quarters. André, like most of the other men, slept on the bottom level, just down from the engine room.

'We'll take it from here,' said one of the women. She was petite with dark brown hair and eyes the colour of the ocean. André blushed as the woman looked at him. He remained by the door long after the nurse closed it. He wanted to ask questions but didn't dare to. What were they planning for this poor girl? He hadn't understood the conversation between Nemo and the priest, but he had recognised the solemn tone.

Back on the bridge the captain was once again at the helm, the pilot dismissed. André took up his position by the echo locator and he watched the trajectory of the submarine as it negotiated through a rocky sub-sea cavern. He had been around the world's oceans at least once during his service to Nemo and yet he did not recall this place at all. Nemo did not need André's help which made him aware that the captain had been this way before. He took in the terrain with curiosity but remained silent and Nemo had already fallen into his usual trance state.

Then, through the huge window, André saw large metallic gates that filled the expanse between two bulky rocks.

'Impossible,' André murmured, unable to help himself.

'An underwater fortress. For an underwater civilisation,' Nemo said. 'This is the entrance to Y'ha-nthlei.'

Nemo slowed the *Nautilus* down to a halt.

'Now what happens?' Asked André.

'We wait. If our visit is welcome the gates will open.'

'And if we are not welcome?'

Nemo didn't answer but his hands tightened on the wheel. Then the gates began to open.

When the entrance was wide, the *Nautilus* edged forward, slower than earlier, as Nemo steered with great care between the gap. André helped to guide the captain using the echo locator to warn him when the sides of the vessel were too close to the rocks.

When the tail of the *Nautilus* passed through the narrow tunnel, the water before them opened up into a new and exciting ocean.

Nemo once again brought the *Nautilus* to a halt.

'Come with me, André,' Nemo said.

The young crewman leapt eagerly from his chair.

Down in the bowels of the ship, a smaller submarine left the *Nautilus*. Inside was the princess taken from the mysterious island, André, two other crewmen and Nemo. Nemo turned the vessel into a narrow gulley that looked like streets submerged under water. Soon they emerged into a clearing – if indeed open water could be likened to that of a space on land – but no other word fit in André's vocabulary for this place. Instead of trees surrounding a space, there were rocks. The place resembled the temple that they had seen on the island, only it was all underwater. Then the *Nautilus*'s small submarine began to rise through the water, and they came up into a large pocket of air.

The crewmen hurried to open the top of the submarine and

then Nemo led the five people out of the submarine and onto the rock face at the side. The air was breathable, but Nemo had known it would be.

'The people of this realm live half in the sea, half on land,' Nemo explained. Then he repeated his explanation in the island language for the benefit of the princess.

Though the girl did not reply she nodded her understanding and she looked around the space with renewed curiosity. André mimicked her expression without realising it. The air smelt salty, but clean and fresh.

Nemo began to climb the rocks and the others followed: André and the princess were behind the captain, while the two crewmen brought up the rear.

They reached a summit and found steps. The princess gasped when she noted the similarity between this temple and her own. She was relaxed, calm, and still showed no sign of fear.

'Come,' Nemo said and she followed, eager now to see what was waiting for them on the top.

The climb was slow, André felt his strength evaporate with every step, yet Nemo appeared to feel no ill effects from being so far below the ocean.

'You'll feel better at the top,' Nemo said and this spurred them all on to climb faster.

At the top the air filled their lungs. It was forest fresh, and André noted the range of plant life that grew from the rocks inside, where an artificial light illuminated the trees and bushes. It was like a magical fairy glen.

'How is this possible?' André asked.

'How does any plant grow?' Nemo said. 'Life adapts. Evolves. The will to survive is in all nature, especially man.'

Sitting on a throne wearing an ornate robe of dark green was a foul sea creature.

The princess immediately prostrated herself before the throne, unafraid, willing. André however found the being so repulsive that he took a step back. At that moment the crewmen caught hold of the young sailor, they dragged him forward, throwing him down at the foot of the throne.

Nemo kneeled beside the princess and the two other men took up position near André, who they watched carefully.

'It must indeed be something important that brings you to our realm,' said the thing on the throne.

It was manlike with two legs, arms, torso, though its head was fish shaped and the scaly skin was dark grey with reptilian density. As it spoke it bared serrated teeth that made André shudder with fear. He didn't know why his crewmen held him down at its feet so brutally; maybe they knew that he would run screaming from this place if they did not. And, he suspected that Nemo would have prepared the others for what they would see. But why hadn't he prepared André? Or was it that the other men had been here with Nemo before?

'Ar'teh Rai,' Nemo said. 'I give you Princess Tembukah to do with as you wish. She is a willing sacrifice.'

'Beautiful too,' Ar'teh Rai replied. 'I have always enjoyed the human female form, so different from our females. The skin is so smooth and soft.'

A thick tongue slithered over rubbery lips and the creature had been speaking for sometime before André realised he could understand its words. The creature's words horrified André – were they going to eat the girl?

'Your tribute is acceptable,' Ar'teh Rai concluded.

Behind the creature's throne emerged three females. They were similar in colour to the monstrosity on the throne, but more human than he appeared: a hybrid of human and this creature. 'Take her to my chamber,' he told the females who now surrounded the princess. Tembukah's eyes were round and filled with adoration as she bowed before the God on the throne. Then she allowed herself to be taken away by the females.

André was now beginning to see what purpose Ar'teh Rai had for the princess, and bile rose in the back of his throat at the thought of this thing using the young girl this way. He turned his head to look at Nemo, and wondered how many such sacrifices had been brought down here in the past. How else would Nemo know the way here without any form of navigation? How else would there be half-breeds?

'And the boy too?' Ar'teh Rai said.

'No …' Nemo shook his head. 'He is a member of my crew …'

'The second sacrifice, as you know, must be unwilling.'

'This young man has a promising career with me as an engineer …' Nemo argued.

'Why have you come here, to merely waste my time?' said Ar'Teh Rai.

'I hoped that a princess would be enough …' Nemo said.

It took a moment for André to realise that they were discussing him. He began to struggle with the two crewmembers that held him.

'No. I won't …' he said.

Ar'teh Rai said, 'His corruption shall be a joy for our females.'

'No!' André cried as several creatures resembling Ar'teh Rai surrounded him. The *Nautilus* crewmen passed him over without a word and then they withdrew to stand to attention behind Nemo.

Nemo remained prostrate before the throne. He could do nothing. This was one sacrifice for the sake of many other lives.

André was dragged. 'Captain! Help me!'

Nemo didn't look at him.

'What do you need,' Ar'teh Rai asked.

'Earth has fallen to our enemies from the stars …'

Ar'teh Rai leaned forward in his throne, 'We felt the tremors, but did not know what it meant. Martians?'

'The priest has confirmed it to be so,' Nemo's voice trembled. He cleared his throat. 'Man cannot fight this. It wears machines and feeds on the blood of humankind.'

'You could have merely fled to the sea. You and your men are safe here. It is after all the life you prefer,' Ar'Teh Rai observed.

'Yes. And my instinct was to do that except … would these beings be satisfied with conquering the land alone? What small leap into the planet's waters it would be for something that has travelled through space.'

Ar'teh Rai was thoughtful, 'What makes you so sure of this? Or that the deep ones could be any form of threat to make this enemy retreat?'

'No one could defeat you on land or in water,' Nemo said. 'Attack before you are attacked. Man did not have the luxury to prepare. But if they had, they still might not have been able to destroy these creatures. Their technology is like nothing I have seen except ... here.'

Nemo's eyes scanned the impossible cavern. Trees, oxygen, plant-life grew in this miracle place, but he knew it was more about technology with the sea gods, rather than magic.

Nemo waited for the king of the deep ones to speak: Ar'teh Rai stood.

He placed a webbed hand on Nemo's shoulder.

'Often you have brought us delights, luxuries in food and human form for us to indulge in. In the old days we would seduce our victims, some willing, others not, making our hybrids, knowing that on birth they would be thrown back into the sea for us to take to our world. As man has evolved, such things had become less attractive, less easy for us to do. The rise of Christianity made demons of gods. It has been some time since we ventured on land.'

'Now that humankind has met a demon from the stars, they will be more susceptible to the revision of old religions. Especially when a real God, like yourself, comes to their rescue,' Nemo said.

'You are wise. And you offer me more in this than the sacrifices we have already accepted. Therefore, I cannot refuse your request. We will emerge from the deep once more and take the land back.'

The *Nautilus* waited just off shore, but still submerged from the eyes of the alien machines while the deep ones, a warrior race from the sea, climbed up from the water and swarmed in their thousands onto London's dockland.

Even on land the beings were agile. One of the creatures leaped into the air, climbing onto the bulbous body of a heat ray machine. It tore at the metal with clawed webbed hands, ripping open the alien's outer shell. Oxygen poured inside, the machine tottered, but the alien didn't fall, instead one of its appendages caught hold of the sea warrior from the top of its machine and then, pierced him with the sharp long needle.

Blue blood came from the creature, not red, but the alien didn't care as it tossed the lifeless warrior aside and injected itself with the blood.

The machine swayed as the alien fed. It took another step, reaching out for one of the warriors that now swarmed around its tripod legs. But the deep ones toppled the being, sending it crashing down hard. The metal casing that covered its body cracked open like an egg. The creature oozed from it. Now unprotected it began to shrivel under the intense rays of the sun. Oxygen pressed against its slimy bulk.

Then the creature bloated and burst: it was an extreme case of the bends.

Several machines appeared on the horizon. They poured towards the docklands as more of the deep ones, including some of their hybrid offspring, continued their assault. Warriors fell and were fed on by the Martians, but each time, the tripod beasts became unsteady and were toppled soon after. It wasn't certain whether the blood of the old sea gods or the exposure to earth's atmosphere was the cause of the combustion but in each case this is how the alien monsters died.

The remaining machines fell back when it became evident that they could not defeat the sea creatures. Even their powerful heat rays, which poured devastation on the landscape, could not boil the ice cold blood of the ancients.

The sea gods poured inland after them, they worked together like soldier ants, using strength and body mass to swarm the final remaining machines.

The battle went on for days, many of the deep ones' warriors died, but their sacrifice was crucial to the survival of the rest.

When England was free, and the remaining population came out of their hovel hiding places, the Sea Gods took any offered sacrifices. Many women came to them willingly, and the rewards for their efforts were reaped over and over again as the warriors lay with them. Then, with instruction on how to deal with hybrid offspring from their unions, the warriors returned to the sea.

Nemo followed and watched as France was taken back, and then as the creatures freed Europe.

It took months to push the enemy back but as the *Nautilus* and the deep ones reached the Americas the aliens were dying: poisoned as they were by the taking of blood from animal, human and sea god alike.

The ancient gods, however, enjoyed the final bloodletting as they swept the land, dipping in and out of sea as they went. The scourge of alien invaders fell beneath their might. The alien machines, and Martian bodies were trampled under webbed feet.

Nemo stood on the deck of the *Nautilus* as Ar'teh Rai pulled himself up from the sea. He bowed to the God as he reached the deck.

'Such is not necessary between us,' Ar'teh Rai said.

The deep ones had saved the planet, and the old religion was now re-established - humanity, as Nemo had predicted, saw the sea creatures as their liberators and gods. Who, unlike the Christian god, was a tangible and approachable benefactor. So what if some of their women were expected to birth hybrids? To pair with a god was a privilege not a sacrifice, and all were more than willing to take on the mantle.

'So you will return to Y'ha-nthlei?' Nemo asked.

'In time: when enough young hybrids have been collected. They will go a long way to replenishing our warriors. But for now we are enjoying the land above.'

Nemo nodded. He understood worship; he had seen it briefly in the eyes of André. But he pushed down the remorse he felt at giving the young man to the deep ones. There had been no choice: sacrifices of all kinds must be made to maintain the equilibrium of the world above and below.

Ar'teh Rai said his goodbyes and dived from the deck of the *Nautilus* back into the sea, but Nemo knew the ancient god was making his way back to land. Maybe another sacrifice waited for him, spread eagerly on the sand?

Nemo wondered though, if there would ever be enough hybrids to satisfy the deep ones now, and had he brought in one invader to depose another?

It didn't matter in the end he supposed, after all, mankind had renewed faith that gave them purpose, and if Ar'teh Rai and the warriors from the deep bred enough - and those hybrids bred again with the remaining humans – how much of humanity would be left to worry about?

Down on the bridge, Nemo ordered his men to dive. He couldn't wait to leave the battlefield behind and return to the ocean. He couldn't wait to find once more his peace of mind. But as the *Nautilus* submerged he couldn't help wondering if he had kept, or failed to keep, his promise to the Queen. Were the oceans safe?

# Other Nightmares

# Walking the Dead

Granny died in front of the telly watching her favourite soap. One minute she was keeled over, drool slipping between her false teeth, a last hiss gurgling in her throat and the next she was going about her business like nothing had happened. At first, I was the only one who noticed there was something wrong and, it even took *me* a day or two to realise she was a zombie.

I was eating a Chinese take-out at the time and when I saw dear old granny slump I started yelling as loudly as I could.

'Oh my Gawd. Mum! Granny's pegged it.'

Mum came rushing in of course, but much to her disappointment Granny didn't look any worse off than before, so she clouted me round the ear.

'Fancy getting my hopes up like that, you little bugger.'

The wandering was a bit of a worry at first. If she got outside she couldn't seem to find her way back, but being at home she was, as Mum always said, 'happy as Larry'. Not that I could ever figure out who this 'Larry' was but it didn't seem to matter in the scheme of things.

A few days later I heard about a friend's uncle getting up off the morgue slab just as they were about to cut him open. Then there was the butcher down the road who got trapped in his own fridge over the weekend. When his assistant arrived at work on Monday morning he found him unconscious on the fridge floor, but within minutes he was up and about, preparing orders. It was weird that his wife hadn't claimed him missing but I think she was hoping he'd run off with one of the women he chatted up in the shop.

We were at school when old Mr Chipperton croaked it during the exam. I was picking my nose and flicking the bogies at snobby Billy 'call me William' Price.

'Sir? Sir?' shouted Billy and everyone looked up and around

the room to see what was going on. 'Sir? Someone keeps flicking *things* at me!'

Mr Chipperton didn't move. Everyone knew he liked to take a nap from time to time but he usually reacted quickly when someone spoke. Gemma Smith was the first one to get up and prod him, then I went over and it was just like my old granny, all flaked out and drooly.

'He's dead,' I pointed out. 'Better go and get the Head.'

Gemma took the news in good spirit. Dead things didn't bother her, unlike everyone else. She held the record for being the 'grossest' girl in school - she even dissected a squirrel we once found. She'd flipped out her pocket knife long before the rest of us reached her. I remember it was all full of maggots and Sophie Price threw up on the pavement when she saw them wriggling around in the squirrel's stomach.

Gemma looked at Old Chipperton, pinching and pulling at him until she was satisfied I was right, then ran off to get the head mistress, Ms Havers. The rest of the kids just sat there, watching the body. I think they weren't really sure if it was a joke. I am a bit of a prankster, and I'd roped Gemma in many times to back up some tall tale or other, so it was understandable that they didn't trust us.

A few minutes later Ms Havers came in with the first aider and they had Old Chipperton on the floor giving him mouth to mouth, but clearly nothing could be done.

'Go into the hall,' said Ms Havers to the class.

She sent Gemma back to the office to tell them to call an ambulance and to send someone down to the hall to look after the kids there.

I stayed behind in the class room to act as a runner. Ms Havers was sitting with the body and, as the ambulance men entered the room, Old Chipperton suddenly stood up.

As we all looked on, mouth open with surprise, Mr Chipperton returned to his seat in front of the class and gazed around rather confused.

'Has the bell gone?' he said at which point, Ms Havers, who'd been too stunned to speak at first, began to scream her head off like she'd lost her mind.

You see, she cottoned on pretty quickly that Old Chipperton was actually still dead and not revived. I think it was something to do with the blueness around the mouth and this awful vacant expression he had. Ms Havers picked up a chair and ran at Mr Chipperton. The ambulance men were a bit shocked, but fortunately one of them reacted by taking her down in a rugby tackle. It all got a bit ugly then. Ms Havers kicked one of the men in the crunches and while he was down, heaving his guts up, she somehow managed to untangle herself from the other one. She crawled agilely across the floor and pulled herself up by holding onto Mr Chipperton's desk. Then she reached for the paperweight and attempted to smash in the old man's brains.

The ambulance men took her away and, after giving him the once over, they left Old Chipperton behind.

'Yep,' said the paramedic. 'You're definitely dead. No heart beat or pulse and your colour is decidedly deprived of oxygen.'

'Oh,' said Mr Chipperton. 'What should I do then?'

'Go home and take two aspirins...' answered the other paramedic, now recovered from Ms Havers' well aimed kick. 'That's what we usually recommend when we don't know what else to do.'

Mr Chipperton picked up his hat and coat and headed for the exit as Ms Havers was wheeled away, suitably drugged and strapped down for her own, and Old Chipperton's, safety. At the door Mr Chipperton paused and looked around. I was still at a loss as to what to do, so I stayed at my desk watching the proceedings. I can't say I wasn't alarmed by it all. It was a bit weird. But what I'd noticed with my Granny was that she had carried on just like she hadn't died. Except she didn't eat or go to the toilet anymore, which pleased my mum because at least she wasn't wetting the bed on Saturday night after she'd had her regular bottle of stout. In fact she didn't want her stout at all now. All she wanted to do was shuffle around and watch *Coronation Street.* I always thought you had to be dead to watch that programme anyway...

Mr Chipperton on the other hand seemed to have retained

full use of his speech.

'Are you alright, Sir?' I asked eventually.

'Yes, thank you. Charlie, isn't it?'

'Yes, Sir.'

'I seem to have forgotten my way home.'

'Oh don't worry. My granny does that as well. I'll take you to the office and get the address.'

I didn't mind helping Old Chipperton and I walked him home that night.

School was closed for a few days to help us kids get over the shock of what happened. Ms Havers didn't come back after that. She became one of the 'Hysterics' and as soon as they let her out of hospital she began the anti-dead group ZADPATEY which basically meant, 'Zombies Are Dead People And They Eat You'. What can I say? She is a teacher and they seem to love acronyms no matter how crap they are. But she had some success with it, got a group of followers together, and suddenly there was a campaign against zombies.

The world went to shit a bit after that. More people died, rose again and general panic ensued. When the reports of the dead reviving and then 'walking' started to filter through, the papers and the news channels, as usual, made a meal of it all: implying that zombies were going to make a meal of us. Naturally that led to mass panic.

Of course, I understood why people were scared. It's not every day a group of dead people surround you, reach out and generally groan - sometimes incoherently - that they needed help. The majority of the living were naturally afraid and ran like hell, occasionally bashing in a zombie brain or two for good measure.

'It's a natural survival instinct to run from the unknown,' said our biology teacher. 'People are just like primates when it all comes down to it. And we don't like being around dead bodies - they smell for a start.'

'But, Sir,' I said. 'I haven't noticed anything different about the way the zombies smell ... and as far as I know they haven't actually hurt anyone.'

'Not yet, Charlie my boy,' answered the teacher. 'But give them time...'

'This is crazy,' said Gemma as we hung around the school yard. 'They are talking about closing the school and Old Chipperton isn't allowed on the premises. Personally I'd rather have a zombie sleeping at the front of the class than that dreadful supply teacher.'

'What's wrong with the supply? Other than the usual...' I asked.

'He looks like a paedo.'

'Yeah,' said Billy, who seemed to have toughened up with the thought of a coming apocalypse. 'They'll let anyone teach these days.'

'Did you see Ms Havers on the telly last night?' asked Gemma.

'She's lost it,' I said.

'If you ask me,' said Billy. 'It's racist.'

At that moment I saw a zombie hanging around outside the gates and realised it was Old Chipperton.

'Better take him home,' I said. 'Otherwise someone will mistake him for a flasher again.'

A few days later there were vans travelling up and down the streets picking up the stray zombies. They seemed to like to congregate in the middle of the road, or in malls. Okay, so it was causing an obstruction for drivers, and scaring away the shoppers, but it seemed grossly unfair to me that they were being locked up just for wandering around. It wasn't as if they were causing a riot or damaging people's property.

'What you going to do with that zombie?' I asked one of the soldiers on the rounds.

'We're just taking him away somewhere for his own protection.'

'We've all heard that before,' mumbled Mum and she took my hand – which was *really* embarrassing – and dragged me back home.

We had to hide granny for a while after that, and when she did go out I pretended she was helping *me* find my way home.

The zombie collections were all over the news and Ms Havers loved the attention of rallying the world against the defenceless dead. The crowd behind her was screaming and shouting at the cameras, but Ms Havers looked really calm and dignified. Her hair was all loose and wavy and she was actually wearing lots of make-up. I'd never seen her look like that before. It was as though she loved being on camera and was trying really hard to be a celebrity.

'Zombies are a danger to us all,' she said calmly. 'Fortunately the security services have now recognised that danger and are beginning to remove this threat from our streets.'

'Ms Havers?' shouted a man from the crowd. 'Do you know what they are *doing* to our dead relatives?'

'Well, if they've any sense they'll put a bullet clean through their dead brains and put them down permanently.'

That's when the riot broke out and the camera was jostled, the news reporter was knocked over and Ms Havers was dived on by an entire mob of unhappy families whose dead had been incarcerated.

It was only natural that a new campaign started soon after. This group was called FreeZom which was obviously a play on the words 'Freedom' and 'Zombies'. FreeZom's campaign became popular within days. No one wanted their dead shot through the brain without first proving they were dangerous. Also, people quickly realised that if nature decided their time was up, they'd rise again as well, and the first thing they'd see when they came round would be the barrel of a soldier's rifle. As if the thought of dying when you *didn't* know what would happen wasn't bad enough! So naturally FreeZom got support from many people. Even those in high places. It was rumoured that Prince Philip was giving financial support to the cause. This did give rise to some speculation that the Queen may already be among the dead and he just wasn't admitting it: but other than the usual wan expression and constantly waving hand - which was the same for all public appearances for years anyway - there really wasn't much evidence to support this view.

Walking back from school was a bit like travelling through a warzone. There were demonstrations on every street corner. One day I came across FreeZom and ZADPATEY on the opposite sides of the road. Some soldiers were trying to round up a small group of zombies who'd congregated in the middle of the street.

'I can't find my way home,' said one of the zombies. She was a small child with a blood stain down the front of her dress. She was dragging her leg, ankle all twisted the wrong way and her arm looked like it was dangling down at her side.

'I'll help you,' said one of the men from ZADPATEY to the little girl.

'Stay away from that zombie child you murdering freak!' shouted a woman from FreeZom as she ran out into the street.

The creepy guy from ZADPATEY made a grab for the poor zombie who screamed and ran, well sort of shambled really, and hid behind the army truck.

A riot broke out between the two factions as they surged across the street converging in the middle of the road.

'Bloody hell,' said a soldier. 'Not again.'

The soldiers waded in, trying to break up the fight. This was good news for the zombies they were trying to round up, of course, and they took the opportunity to wander away from the trouble and stumble back home - if they could find it.

I took the zombie girl's hand and led her away as fast as her trailing leg could manage. Around the next corner we found her bike, all crushed and bloody.

'Did someone knock you over?' I asked.

'Yep. Next door neighbour... Then, when I woke up, he rang the soldiers to come and get me,' she said.

'Harsh.'

We found the little girl's mother beating the neighbour around the head with a broken umbrella.

'Just wait till one of your family dies. It wasn't bad enough that you ran my girl down; you had to turn her in as well. You murdering bastard!'

The neighbour skulked away when the kid's mother saw her broken child limping towards her.

'Thank you so much,' cried the mother who turned out to be

a nurse. She quickly popped her daughter's dislocated shoulder back into place. 'Come inside and we'll patch up that leg ...'

'Best put an address label on her from now on,' I suggested.

I watched them go in doors. It gave me a strangely peculiar feeling of satisfaction that I'd helped them. I turned around and went home, hoping that one day someone would do the same for me.

That night *Corrie* was interrupted by a news flash. Granny got mega irritated and started pacing the room as her routine was completely disrupted.

*'Investigators into the recent outbreak of the zombie virus been taken to the court of European Rights today. After a long hearing and a thorough examination of all evidence it has been ruled that there is no indication that zombies are dangerous and imprisonment of the dead is unlawful. The court granted zombies limited citizenship. This is good news for the FreeZom Campaigners as all zombies are to be returned to their families as soon as possible,'* the reporter said.

'It's a trap,' said Mum. 'They are hoping we'll let out our relatives again so they can round them up.'

'Shush. I'm trying to hear this,' I said, then ducked as Mum automatically swung her arm to give me a clout.

*'Furthermore the court ruled that any attempt to smash in a zombie's head will be considered assault.'*

At that moment the camera switched to a group of protestors. Ms Havers jumped forward and grabbed the microphone from the reporter's hand. 'We at ZADPATEY believe that zombies are evil. Don't be fooled people. They are just waiting for an opportunity to EAT YOUR BRAINS!'

The reporter pulled his microphone away and the police came forward to push Ms Havers and her followers back.

'Lock your doors. Don't go out until this plague is destroyed.' yelled Ms Havers. 'I implore you ... hit your dead over the head before they make a meal of you.'

'Brains?' said Granny as she sat down before the telly again. 'I'm a vegetarian...'

I looked at Mum and she squirmed a bit but didn't say

anything. It wasn't usual these days for Granny to make much comment, but she was clearly still following what was happening in the world.

'Want some stout, Granny?' I asked later but she was zonked out in the chair, feet stretched out towards the telly.

The living room was freezing cold. We were wrapped up in sweaters and coats because we couldn't put the heating on.

'Mum?' I said later. 'What are we going to do if she starts to smell a bit?'

'I don't know,' said mum. 'I'm trying to preserve her as best as I can. But I never thought I'd have this problem, always thought I'd shove her in a home when she got on my nerves too much. But I like her much better since she became a zombie. She's far less trouble.'

After a few weeks, the madness calmed down and the dead returned to the streets once more. As I went past the local burial service I noticed they had a new sign up. Last week they'd announced redundancies and closures since no one was burying their dead anymore. But now, there was a sign saying: GET YOUR DEAD EMBALMED TODAY.

When I got home, I noticed Granny was looking rather well. Her hair was brushed, false teeth polished and her skin had taken on a healthy glow.

'Get you,' I said.

'Been embalmed,' she mumbled, and then she sat down and pressed the remote control.

'Nice one,' I said.

'Will you take her out for a walk?' Mum asked later. 'She does so love to walk, but I don't like to let her out alone as she still hasn't learnt her way back home.'

A few minutes later we were shuffling proudly through the streets as Granny was showing off her new look to the other zombies.

'That looks good. Wonder if my wife will let me be embalmed,' said the butcher.

'Go home and ask her,' I suggested.

'Can't,' he said shaking his head sadly. 'Don't know the way.'

Luckily I remembered that they lived above his shop and Granny and I took him home. On the way back we helped a few more lost zombies.

'They really should wear address labels...' I said to Mum when we got back home.

Granny was really perky after the walk and we all played a game of scrabble. Of course her spelling was rubbish but Mum and I accepted her versions of words without argument. It was nice to be doing something so normal with her again.

The next day at school I joined Gemma and Billy in the canteen.

'The way I see it, there's a need for a service in this community. I've got an idea if you two fancy earning some money with me,' I said. 'Let's set up a walking service.'

'Urgh! I hate dogs,' said Gemma.

'I don't mean a *dog* walking service – I mean zombies.'

Billy started to laugh, almost choking on his beef sandwich, 'You're joking right?'

'I think that's a great idea,' said Gemma. 'I like the dead. We could all do with the extra money; and it's kind, as well. How do you think we should do this?'

I explained my plan and later that day in art, we made a poster advertising our services, and then photocopied it in the staff room while the teachers were outside smoking behind the bike sheds. On the way home we attached posters to lamp posts and walls.

It wasn't long before our service was taken up by locals with wandering dead relatives. We soon had a regular client list, and it stopped the random walking that had scared so many people. We discovered that walking the dead made them feel much better. It seemed restored some of their basic thought and motor skills. It was why they liked to go out and walk around so much. It made them feel more alive again.

Within a few months Gemma, Billy and I had too much work on our hands so we roped in a few more kids.

'I don't know how you can do it,' yelled Ms Havers as we passed her on the street.

We ignored her. She was just scum to us. After all she had an ASBO and a restraining order to keep her away from all zombies. I believed it was the only thing stopping her from whacking as many on the head as she could.

'It's people like you that give education a bad name,' Billy shouted as all three of us walked past her. She was always hanging around the off licence, now, holding a bottle in a brown paper bag. Her hair was wild, clothes unwashed and she looked more dangerous to us than our zombie clients ever could have.

When I got home that night I found Mum and Granny sitting together in the lounge.

'I finally found something she likes to drink,' said Mum and for the first time in ages she looked truly excited. 'I picked up a supply of embalming fluid to top her up and found her slurping from the jar through a straw.'

'Its good shit this stuff,' said Granny. 'Wanna try some?'

'No, thanks. Don't think it would agree with me. Maybe in a few years time when I'm a zombie.'

'Just hope she doesn't start peeing in the bed again,' Mum said. 'I'd never get that yellow stain out of the sheets.'

It didn't take long for a few more zombies to realise that drinking embalming fluid was fun and it gave them energy.

After that the zombies founded their own bars and clubs. You could see them sitting in roadside cafes drinking yellow gloop from fancy china. Granny joined a zombie group that met once a week and she regained a whole new lease on life. After all, she may have been dead and old but she no longer suffered from the aches and pains she once had before she died. She was, in fact, quite spritely these days.

It just goes to show you though; it all could have turned out so differently if we had listened to Ms Havers. My mum says it's George Romero's fault that we all thought the worst. Sometimes the cinemas show re-runs of the movies – they are all considered comedies and the zombies attend them in droves laughing at the absurdity.

'Why on earth would we want to eat brains,' said the butcher, 'when embalming fluid is so very, very good?'

I took the bag containing mum's meat order and paid him with my hard earned 'walking money'.

Billy, Gemma and I gave up school to run our Walking the Dead business. There really wasn't much point in continuing our education when we had a sure career already established, one that wasn't going to run out of clients anytime soon. Besides, the authorities were too busy arguing about the zombies to worry about a bunch of kids bunking off school.

There still are debates on telly about the ever-growing zombie population. Mum says the discussions will go on for ages, but I don't care about that. They've had a bad press for years. Some people say there's been a strange twist of fate, and that the zombies have turned out to be our future and shouldn't be feared. Mum says the jury's still out on that. But until someone proves otherwise I'll go on walking the dead.

# The Last Resort

As they wheeled him over the threshold, Charlie Ericson knew that he wouldn't be leaving. The last resort was a downtown hospital. The big C had finally caught up with him. and he was going down after a battle that had cost him both wealth and dignity.

Charlie had money, all the money he would ever need for several lifetimes, let alone this one, and he had spent a good deal of it on doctors and medication since he received the bad news. He had lived on a cocktail of pills, injections and chemo therapy and had endured painful surgery - all to no avail.

His wife, Jasmine, had cried suitably when he told her, but he had seen the 'look' beneath the tears. She knew her time had finally come to inherit everything *he* had worked for. He didn't mind though. She was young, but she had been a good wife the last five years, doing everything he said, and always being wonderfully well-groomed, just as he wanted her to be. He didn't mind paying for all the beauty treatments, clothes, hair and nail appointments, that was all part of having such a beautiful trophy on his arm. And Charlie liked trophies.

Charlie collected things: expensive art; rare wines; one-of-a-kind masterpieces of all descriptions; filling his several houses with these wonders because he enjoyed beautiful objects. It all meant nothing in the end though. There are no pockets in shrouds - a truer phrase had never been coined. *Still,* he reflected, *it's been a good life and I did my best.*

A nurse placed an oxygen mask over his mouth and nose and someone opened his shirt and began pressing the small disks attached to the heart monitor onto his chest. Charlie felt it, but the pressure was distant as his mind floated in a morphine-induced daze. He felt no pain, only a warm certainty that this was final. The End.

He floated. It was a lovely cosy feeling, like the moment when you are half-asleep, when you feel relaxed and safe. Charlie let his thoughts glide too. It even occurred to him that he was reliving his life, seeing it all before his eyes at his concluding moment. That was a good thing though wasn't it? Surely he had no regrets.

He saw Jasmine, looking radiant on their wedding day. She was beautiful to the point of breath-taking. Hadn't he always thought that? She was something he had to acquire, and it hadn't been easy convincing her to leave her medical practice, after all that hard work. She was smart, he knew that, respected it, but had never had any need for it. He wanted her to be a woman, a goddess that he could put up on a pedestal, and she had never disappointed him.

'I'm here, Charlie,' she said beside him, as though she could feel the thoughts, or maybe he had said her name aloud as he thought of her.

He tried to open his eyes: they felt sticky and sandy all at the same time.

He felt her hand on him, stroking, patting, there was love in it. Or at least he chose to believe there was. He could never be sure though, why she had married him.

Charlie drew in a shallow breath, it hurt and his chest felt tight while his lungs screamed and he heard a sharp sound pierce the air.

'He's in pain,' said Jasmine. 'Can't you help him?'

'We're giving him as much as we can,' said the nurse. 'He won't suffer for long now.'

Charlie felt a small spike of fear. What would the afterlife be like? Was there a Hell? He had never really believed in any of that, though he had never disbelieved either. He had always known that this moment would arrive, but even when he was diagnosed with Cancer (and the word had to have a capital letter) he still refused to think that the end would arrive. And he had fought it. He really had.

It was hard to imagine not existing any more. Not owning his treasures.

Jasmine had cried so much when he told her. She'd had frequent nightmares afterwards, but it couldn't change anything. His death, with her love or without it, had touched them both. There was no avoiding the obvious truth that the end comes to us all. Mortality was such a fleeting thing.

'Charlie,' she said. 'I should have told you the truth. Everything about me.'

Charlie's mind snapped back to the present. What did she say? His eyes fluttered again. He could see Jasmine through the slits, and sensed that they were now alone. The morphine was wearing off and pain worked its way around the edges of his consciousness.

'I lied when I said I could accept being childless,' Jasmine confided. 'I wanted our child.'

Charlie wasn't surprised by this revelation. He had known that at some point the old biological clock would kick in for Jasmine. It had happened with his last two wives. Each divorce had cost him a chunk of his estate, but Charlie had always recovered, and years later when he had seen the mess that childbirth had made of the perfection that once was, his resolve to never be a father had strengthened. Perfection was all he required from a wife, even if that meant surgery to maintain it. And he was always willing to pay for that kind of maintenance.

Jasmine had been most diligent about keeping fit, eating the right foods, while all the time indulging Charlie's wishes. She had never once mentioned children. In fact she complained when they came across the noisy little brutes in restaurants. Although the kind of restaurants they ate in rarely permitted that kind of disruption to the peace and quiet of their regular clients, and parents with rowdy offspring were politely asked to leave.

Charlie remembered one such incident when Jasmine had protested to the management in their favourite Italian. They boasted of exclusivity for their fine guests. But then there had been that one family they allowed in. Jasmine had ensured that the entire group was removed just because a child dropped his fork noisily down onto his plate. He had thought she hated children and it seemed a little excessive at the time. Now he considered it, he realised that Jasmine didn't want to be faced with the one thing she could never have.

'Do you believe in life after death,' she had asked him once.

'No, and I'm sure that someone with your background in science doesn't either,' Charlie had said, and the conversation was closed.

'I couldn't talk to you about anything,' Jasmine said. She was still squeezing his hand. 'Not even that I really do care about you. Not that I'm sure you believe that. It's true though Charlie. I wish I could wave a magic wand and take all of this away.'

Charlie sighed into the plastic mask. It was nice of her to say the right things; she was so good at that. Probably it would assuage any guilt she would feel after his death. She had done her best, and cared for him the way he asked to be cared for. Charlie couldn't have asked for more.

'Of course I know what you did,' Jasmine said. 'About those two women.'

Charlie's mind turned these words over. Did she believe he had been having an affair? Or multiple affairs? He would never have done that to her. He had needed no one else.

'You like your trophies, I understand that. But it wasn't fair of you to lie about the children.'

Charlie wasn't sure where this was going. What did she mean?

'Those two women who had your kids. The ones you refused to acknowledge.'

*Ah.*

'If you had fathered them, why didn't you care what happened?'

*Of course,* Charlie remembered.

A slight glitch in his psyche. He had lost his mind for a short time. The news of his possible demise three years ago had come as something of a trauma. Panic had set in when he realised that all he was, all he had been, would one day just disappear. There was Jasmine, supportive, beautiful and perfect. He couldn't ask her for the one thing he had said he would never need. He had let the idea fly unchecked through his mind for a week or two, then Jasmine had begun to feel sick, complaining of a pain in her side. She was rushed into hospital and while he was undergoing chemo, Jasmine underwent surgery for acute appendicitis.

Charlie had expressed concern about the scar and damage to her flat stomach. Then, when she had healed, and Charlie had thought he had beaten the disease, he had persuaded her to undergo further surgery to improve the damage.

At the time she had agreed, not knowing Charlie's real motives. He had arranged it all discretely. Money can buy you anything, even the loyalty of a doctor. Jasmine went in for the tummy tuck, but the plastic surgeon had only taken over after the gynaecologist had neatly removed the ovum that Charlie wanted.

They had stored her eggs for a while before the surrogates were found. Charlie had already given the sample needed before the chemo destroyed his sperm, making him infertile, and Jasmine need never know that he had left a piece of himself behind in a medical freezer.

'It wasn't just you though, was it?' Jasmine said. 'You made a decision that involved me too.'

*I did what I thought was right! I couldn't ruin you. I couldn't go to my grave after that destruction.*

Her hand felt cold in his now. It was as though she disagreed with him. Charlie felt a pain deep inside his chest that had nothing to do with the lung cancer.

'I'm adopting them, Charlie. Those two little girls. My daughters. You made them in both of our image and I can give them so much of your wealth. Everything children of ours would deserve.'

Charlie squeezed his eyes shut, then tried to open them again. He wondered how she had found out. He had used the best people, spent good money for silence.

'Who?' he said. His voice was little more than a whispered croak.

Jasmine leant over him, raised his head and lifted the mask

enough so that she could offer the glass of tepid water to his lips.

'The doctor you used, Eric Shelman. He and I studied together. He was a brilliant young surgeon. When he saw me asleep and realised who I was he felt tremendous guilt at taking the money. The only way he could redeem himself was by telling me the truth. Of how you used those women…'

'They were paid…' Charlie said.

'Yes. But these were our children, Charlie. How could you leave them with two women who didn't care?'

She laid him back gently on the bed and replaced the mask. Then she stood, went to the sink beside the bed and dampened a paper towel.

'Here,' she said. Then she wiped the gloop from his eyes.

Charlie blinked. It was more comfortable now. He could actually open his eyes a little more and look at Jasmine.

She was immaculate as always. Make-up, hair, nails all neat and beautiful. She smiled at him and then he saw the nurse come in behind her.

'Time for another injection,' said the nurse.

Jasmine held his hand as the nurse fed more morphine into his drip. He felt the immediate rush into his vein, and the wooziness as the crouching pain, and the world, diminished again.

He remembered the day he first saw Jasmine. He had still been married to his second wife at the time, but there were grumblings and she wasn't taking quite the same care of herself as she had in the early days. Charlie had noticed fine lines across her brow but Melissa had been squeamish about injections and had refused the Botox he suggested she have. He was never forceful with his suggestions, but still he had expected her to take the hint.

Jasmine was working as an intern at the hospital. Even in her doctor's scrubs she looked magnificent, not a hair out of place, and Charlie had known he could mould her even more if she would prove to be the type. He didn't act on it then; he waited until Melissa put a few more nails in her own coffin. The late night binges, the excessive consumption of alcohol when they were out with friends, and the final, most unforgivable crime: asking to have a child.

Melissa was paid off quickly after that. Charlie could almost see that this had been her plan all along but he had no regrets, moving on to begin his courtship of Jasmine. Once she had agreed to marry him, and signed the pre-nuptial, everything had gone Charlie's way from then on.

'Of course there has only ever been your way,' said Jasmine. 'You can see how wrong it was to be so controlling can't you?'

He tried to respond but his tongue felt thick and the words wouldn't form on his lips. Already half-dead, Charlie drifted on the dream of perfection. His many treasures passed by as though they were on a conveyor belt, but Jasmine was there in the spot that said 'Most Treasured.' And it was true. Looking back along the line he saw Melissa and Anna as mere possessions he had bought and resold at a loss he was glad to absorb.

Didn't it say something that he had chosen Jasmine to have his children, even though he hadn't told her? She was, and would be, always his favourite.

Over the years he had refused to see his own faults, but maybe he had been an idiot this time.

He opened his eyes a little once more. The light was shining on Jasmine, but this time her face was far less perfect. *This is what you might look like in twenty years,* he thought. *At least I won't have to see your perfection deteriorate.*

He closed his eyes again. He dreamed of walks in the park. Two old farts, happy to be feeding the ducks. But Charlie's life had never been that simple. He couldn't see himself really accepting old age gracefully like a worn down cliché.

His lungs heaved again. Pain like hot coals sat on his chest, burning their nova flame through to his heart.

The chance had gone for good now. And his future was no longer a viable prospect. He accepted it finally, even though he wasn't ready to give up on the images he was seeing of an alternative future.

He heard the sharp sound again. Felt Jasmine's hand on his. She was squeezing as though she were trying to hold onto him.

*I made a mistake,* he thought. *You're right I should have given you the choice. You would have made a wonderful mother.*

Jasmine gasped a small 'no' and Charlie slipped away. He heard the machine's incessant bleeping turn into a flat tone as he drifted upwards, away from his body.

'Jasmine?'

'Eric. I didn't know *you* worked here,' Jasmine said, looking up as she waited in the corridor for the coroner.

'I've worked here for some years now,' Eric Shelman said.

'Really?'

'This may not be the right time... I heard about your husband. I'm sorry,' Eric said.

'Eric. No, please. I'd be glad to talk a while. It will take my mind off things. So you are in private medicine now.'

'Yes. I wanted to talk to you about what I do.'

Jasmine frowned. 'I'm not working as a doctor anymore.'

'I know. In fact I know a lot about a lot of things that I... Look, please come to my office. I have something very important to tell you.'

She followed him down the corridor, not knowing that Charlie was there too. He had been with her since he had parted ways with his body. At first he had tried to talk to her, reassure her as she sobbed, head down, on the empty shell which had been his body.

In his office, Eric offered her coffee, which she took politely even though she normally never drank it.

'I'm sorry about Charlie,' he said again.

'Me too. Just six months ago we thought we had this beaten. Then it seemed to come back with a vengeance,' Jasmine said.

'Cancer can be like that.'

'I knew Charlie,' Eric said. 'I worked for him once.'

Jasmine frowned again as she sipped the coffee. 'Oh? But I

thought you only did…'

'I'm still a gynaecologist. You see, the prospect of death can do strange things to the human mind. I was happy to help him at the time. But that was before I knew you were his wife.'

Jasmine's cheeks were pale. She looked like a woman standing on the edge of a precipice, who knew that any moment she would fall, yet would have no way of stopping herself.

'I don't… understand.'

'Three years ago, Charlie brought you into this hospital for an operation…'

Then Eric told Jasmine about the time he had helped Charlie, three years before. When she finally left his office, a few hours later, she had the name and address of two women.

'It's up to you what you do,' said Eric. 'We were friends at med school. I've tortured myself about this ever since.'

Charlie followed Jasmine back to the coroner's office. His thoughts were confused. He must have imagined the conversation they had about the children. Maybe some guilt had slipped into those final moments? Yes. He should have told her himself in the end and didn't understand why he hadn't. *We do such strange things in life,* he thought. *But I loved you Jasmine. I wanted you to live on with me.*

'Dr Franks? I'm Mrs Ericson,' Jasmine said as the door opened.

'Mrs Ericson, do come in.'

The door closed but it was only a thought that took him through to the other side. Charlie felt that he couldn't leave her. He had to know she was all right.

'The reason I called you here is that we have discovered that your husband is a perfect match for a heart transplant patient we have. I know this may seem insensitive right now, but some good could come out of his death. He could save someone else's life.'

*No!* Thought Charlie, *I've always hated the idea of being a donor.*

Jasmine looked at her hands as they rested in her lap. She said nothing for a while but Charlie was certain she would refuse. She would never go against his wishes on this.

'My husband always wanted me to donate his body to medical science,' she said. 'He even mentioned it in his final moments. I'm not all that keen on the idea but I would never go against his wishes. You may do what you need to his body. I don't believe he is still in there anyway.'

Charlie screamed but no one heard him. His ethereal body beat against the desk without impact. He swiped at the papers as he watched Jasmine sign the consent form, but he realised that he had no shape or form, only knowledge, sight and hearing.

He plummeted, losing control of his direction. When he tried to follow Jasmine, he found that he couldn't leave the hospital. His feet became glued every time he made an attempt to cross the threshold. Eventually, after several failed attempts to move forward, he stood in the doorway watching her walk out to the limo. He saw his chauffeur open the door for her, and what shocked him most was how she tugged her hair free of the severe bun, shaking it out over her shoulders like some street harlot.

The limo drove away and so, not knowing where else to go, Charlie went in search of his body.

He found himself in a fridge in the basement, lying on a cold trolley like a piece of discarded meat. He was naked under a white sheet, his body had been washed and his heart removed. There was a huge wound down the front of his chest, roughly sewn together. Not the neat stitches of a surgeon who cared.

He floated over himself, wondering what to do. Was this it? Was this the afterlife? Where was the tunnel? The light? Where were the burning fires of Hell or the musical world of Heaven? If this was all there was, then perhaps Hell would have been a better place to be.

Charlie drifted out as the fridge door opened and his body was pulled free. He could see his still handsome face. He looked as though he were sleeping.

'Well done, Eric,' said Doctor Franks. 'This is an excellent specimen. I've already implanted, so now we need to get the body out of here.'

*Where are you taking me?* asked Charlie. *What implant?*

'Well I knew when I told her the truth she would want her revenge. Who wouldn't?' said Eric.

'You never did tell me when and how you gave him the cancer cells though. That was a stroke of genius,' Franks said.

'He was obsessed with his health. He had pure oxygen circulated into his office. I just made sure that the canister was changed when I knew he was there alone. He breathed it in, just as surely as he would have breathed in nicotine had he been a smoker. Two hours is all it took and then months of incubation in those lungs did the rest of the job.'

'Naturally the chemo didn't work,' smiled Franks.

'Placebos,' Eric confirmed. 'Pure saline injections, sugar coated aspirin ... you know the score.'

The door to the mortuary opened and an orderly came in.

'Just in time,' said Franks. 'This one is to be placed in the ambulance to my clinic just outside.'

The orderly pushed the trolley towards the door. Charlie followed as though compelled to remain by its side and so did Eric Shelman.

He saw his body loaded into the back of the ambulance, and then floated inside as Eric sat down beside him. The orderly closed the doors.

'Ready?' said Franks from the front seat.

'Definitely. We should hurry though. Colour's starting to return to his cheeks. He's going to start coming around at any time and we don't need that to happen until we can get him sedated and hooked up to the life support machines.'

The ambulance moved off. Charlie was confused. He was dead. How could he possibly come round? He abruptly zoned out. Blessed darkness took him like sleep and he could hear no more.

A warm rush of sensation and feeling came back into his body. He felt pins and needles. Charlie blinked. He tried to run his tongue over dry cracked lips, only to feel the chocking pressure of a plastic tube that had been fed down his throat. His eyes fluttered and panic flooded his body as he felt himself choking. The sensation was worse than death had been.

'How's the patient?' Franks asked, his voice muffled at first, and then clearing.

'Drugged enough not to feel anything. That is if there is any brain capacity left after being clinically dead for several hours,' said Eric.

Charlie opened his eyes slightly, peering through the slit. He tried not to gag on the tube and concentrated on calming his breathing as he took in his environment. This looked like an operating theatre, but Charlie couldn't be sure.

'Well he certainly kept himself fit. This is an ideal specimen,' Franks said.

'How's the implant looking,' asked Eric.

'All good. The tissue has grafted well. He's a perfect incubator.'

Charlie opened his eyes a little more. Above him was a monstrous painting on the ceiling. It was of some hideous creature, naked and covered in sores, with a swollen lump protruding from his chest. The monster was wired up to several machines. He recognised a heart monitor, and the oxygen and life support devices that had been around him in the hospital.

He squeezed his eyes shut. *Why would anyone put such a horrible image up on a ceiling?* He drifted in and out of sleep. Confusion and medication was clearly making him hallucinate. He hadn't died after all.

Where was Jasmine? Why wasn't she at his side like a good wife should be?

When he opened his eyes again the monster was still there, only this time he could see Doctor Franks and Doctor Shelman too. They were in scrubs and masks and wearing rubber gloves as though they were prepared for surgery.

'Have you got a Petri dish ready?' asked Eric.

Franks held out the plastic pot as Eric began to slice into the distorted mass with a scalpel. Charlie felt a momentary discomfort, a tugging sensation that quickly developed into a sharp pain. He watched as Eric lowered a slither of skin into the dish.

The heart monitor spiked.

'What was that?' asked Franks as he placed the lid on the dish. He put it down beside him on the surgical trolley.

'Slight spike. Nothing serious. Doesn't matter anyway, he's brain-dead.'

Charlie began to make sense of the image. He was looking up at a polished steel ceiling. His mind began to scream, while his throat gagged and choked again on the tube. He tried to move his arms but his limbs were paralysed or tied down, he wasn't sure. But he knew what the thing was now. He recognised the eyes in the bloated face.

'Let's take a sample from the face,' Franks said.

Franks came into view, blocking out the horrible sight above him. Then Charlie stared in horror as the scalpel came down, cutting out a piece of his swollen cheek.

'Let's hope that this shows up something we can use for an antidote. Those kids don't deserve to suffer,' Eric said.

Charlie felt a scream bubbling inside him again, but it had nowhere to go. As Franks moved away he saw a gaping hole in his face; red blood mixed with oozing yellow pus. His stomach turned.

*This is me,* he thought. *Oh my God this is* me!

He saw it all now, his naked glory exposed to the world. There was a tube in his gangrenous penis, two in his nostrils, and a vile looking substance, black as faeces and as rank as poison, was being pumped out of his body through a shunt in his stomach. He saw what was left of his arms, grotesque stumps that were raggedly sewn off at the shoulder. One leg remained, though it was swollen like a bloated sausage that was ready to burst in a hot pan, while the other was severed at the knee. He felt heat emanating from his flesh. He knew he was rotting from the inside out.

The horror dawned on him even as the reality of his life/death situation sank in: they were taking pieces of him, while keeping him alive. This was what Jasmine had done, perhaps never knowing how deep her revenge would go.

He had spent his entire life looking after his body, only to see cancer eat away at him. A cancer he had been given, not something that had developed on its own. Now they had done this to him.

In his mind's eye he saw Jasmine smiling as she signed the form. The pen scratched. Again. And again. And again. Taking away the rights he had taken for granted all of his life.

# Three Sisters

*'They met me in the day of success: and I have learned by the perfect'st report, they have more in them than mortal knowledge.'*

*Macbeth,* William Shakespeare

'I'm sorry we can't be much help,' said Cara. 'My sisters and I all suffer from a rare visual disorder. It may appear that we can see, but most of our vision is tunnel.'

'I'm sorry to hear that,' said Inspector Philip Peak.

'It's a form of glaucoma,' said Angela. 'It's inherent in our case. Peripheral vision is something that none of us has.'

'Especially if we are all facing forward,' added Elise.

'Yes, I understand,' Peak said.

The three sisters lived next door to the victim. They were similar in looks and, in their own way, were all very beautiful women. Peak couldn't remember the last time he had met women like this. It didn't happen often in his line of work. They were well turned out in smart suits. Hair groomed, faces subtly made up but naturally attractive.

Cara was the most beautiful: her hair was lighter red than the other two and she had one pale white streak running through the front. He had thought she was the eldest of the three and then it came out so casually that they were, in fact, maternal triplets. Of course this meant they weren't identical but Peak could see the similarities even more once he knew. Angela's hair was a few inches shorter than Cara's and Elise's was the darkest red of them all: a pure, dark auburn. If you put them side by side, like a colour chart they demonstrated light, medium and dark, and this extended to their skin tone as well.

They were odd though. Peak noticed that they had a strange way of speaking, as though they were always continuing each other's sentences, and it made him feel slightly unnerved.

At that moment a loud barking noise came from the house of the victim. Peak had already determined that the dog was a Spaniel and that it hadn't stopped barking since the police broke in and found its owner's body. Unfortunately, the dog was so worked up that none of them had been able to get near the corpse to examine it for fear of being bitten.

Cara cringed when she heard the sound.

'We have very acute hearing,' said Angela.

'Which makes loud noises most unpleasant for us,' Elise continued.

'Constant barking is torture,' Cara said.

Peak nodded. 'Not long now and the handler will take the animal away. Did your neighbour have any relatives?'

The triplets didn't answer because at that moment the animal rescue van arrived. Peak couldn't help but notice how the three sisters turned their heads in unison, like a reflex, to look out of the window of their lounge as Mark Daniels jumped from the car. They stared at him down the tunnel of their vision, classically beautiful faces completely blank. Peak was reminded of something he had read or seen somewhere. A similar image of three goddess statues floated in his mind, but he couldn't quite form the image, or remember where it came from.

'I had better go and speak to him,' Peak said.

At the front door his eyes fell on a clear glass bowl. It was full of strange charms on rings, bracelets and key rings. One of the key rings had a pentagram attached that contained a small clear stone at its heart.

'A blood stone,' Cara said. 'Superstition has it as being used in a ritual for binding someone to an unbreakable promise.'

'We research into the paranormal at the university,' Angela said.

'Some people believe very strange things,' finished Elise.

'Hey Phil,' said Daniels as Peak came out of the house.

'Mark,' Peak nodded. 'The dog is still inside there.'

'Spaniel?' Daniels asked.

'Yeah. Nasty little beggar to be honest.'

Peak pulled Daniels closer to the door to be out of earshot from the sisters.

'So what's the situation?' Daniels said.

'Looks like the owner died and the dog has been chowing down on the body. It's fairly ugly in there. According to the neighbours the dog has been barking non-stop for the last few days. That's why they alerted us.'

'Okay. Leave it to me,' Daniels said.

Daniels went inside and more loud barking ensued. Peak glanced at the sisters. All of them, particularly Cara, appeared to be in a great deal of pain. The women huddled together as though this were the most terrible sound they had ever heard. Then the dog yelped. Cara jumped, Angela and Elise jumped a fraction of second behind her. Then all three sighed as the dog was silenced.

Daniels came out a few minutes later carrying the animal.

'Had to drug it. Too far gone.'

Peak nodded. He knew then that even if there were relatives this dog could not be housed now. There was only one place it was going and that was straight to the vet to be put out of its misery. But of course there were procedures to be followed first, it was never that simple and they would have to find out more about the victim anyway. Whether there were relatives or dependents, that sort of thing.

Peak's forensic team entered the house. He glanced back at the triplets and saw they were watching Mark load the dog into the van. They were all smiling. Peak had never seen such a change in demeanour in a matter of seconds. They appeared to be relieved and, for the first time since he met them, relaxed.

*I guess that dog really was annoying,* he thought.

Cara turned her head to look at him a fraction of a second before the other two. It was strange how they did that. As if they received some kind of subliminal message from each other. Peak nodded, Cara gave him a beautiful smile. She had perfect teeth, and her green eyes were slightly brighter than her sisters'. The other women just stared. Then, the three sisters turned and went back into their house.

Peak noted how the victim was the opposite of the young and pretty women she lived next door to. This woman was overweight and in her fifties. She was wearing a bright fuchsia top and three quarter leggings that would have done nothing to flatter her extreme curves. Sports clothing, worn by someone who clearly didn't look after herself, was always something Peak had thought was paradoxical.

She was lying on her front, bare calves facing upwards and this is where the dog had fed from the most. It was as though the bloated flesh had been a tasty morsel. Peak felt sick, but tried to hide it from the forensic doctor and the other police officers. Squeamishness was something that soon got around in the station, and he couldn't bear the thought of being the brunt of all of those dead body jokes. He detached himself from the thought that this had once been a human. The bruised, torn flesh around the calves looked like overripe tomatoes that had burst as they rotted. The dog had worried at her forearm too, biting through the ugly top and ripping into the podgy skin beneath. Peak's eyes travelled upwards. Her face was turned towards him. There was a thick black bruise and a smear of blood on her forehead.

'Looks like she fell and couldn't get up again,' Doctor Shaw said. 'May have knocked herself out. Awful way to go.'

Peak agreed. It was a terrible thing to turn into your own dog's dinner. He hoped that she had been dead before the meal started.

They took photos - not that Peak would ever have trouble remembering the details of this one - and Shaw took the temperature of the corpse and checked the flexibility of its limbs and the pooling of the blood in the lowest regions.

'Three days is my guess,' Shaw said.

'That fits in with the length of time the dog was barking,' Peak said. 'Must have driven the neighbours crazy.'

Peak went outside. He looked around the back, checking the

windows and doors. It was all routine though because this case was going to close for certain with the conclusion that the victim had fallen and died. There was no evidence to say it was any more sinister than that. He found a window open in the downstairs bathroom, but it was so tiny that he couldn't imagine anyone being able to pass through it. Even so, he took some photographs for later reference.

Then he saw the neighbour on the other side waving over the fence at him. She was a black woman in her sixties. Smart, well-turned out. Sophisticated. This was obviously a nice neighbourhood. The kind his wife aspired to. He glanced at the back door of the victim's house. He couldn't imagine the dead woman fitting in here at all.

'Hello,' he said.

'Can I make you officers some tea?'

'That's very kind of you, but what I'd really like is to ask you some questions.'

The woman nodded, 'Of course, officer. Please come round.'

The front door was open when he reached it and the woman waited for him.

'Margaret Beech. Pleased to meet you Inspector Peak. Do come in,' she said.

Peak wasn't too surprised that she knew his name already. Anyone that he had spoken to so far could have told her.

Margaret led him into the kitchen. It wasn't dissimilar to the victim's but somehow it had more taste.

'This is a respectable neighbourhood,' Margaret said. 'Janice wasn't one of us, but I'm sorry about what has happened. No one deserves that.'

'Deserves what?' asked Peak.

'I heard one of your men saying that the dog …'

Peak let the sentence hang in the air but didn't confirm Margaret's suspicions.

'Can you tell me a little about her?' he asked instead.

'She was fairly friendly when she moved in. But it became evident almost immediately that she wasn't our sort.'

'What do you mean?'

'Well her friends for a start. All that coming and going on motorbikes and the cars arriving at all hours. Then the dog of course. She frequently left it locked in there for hours on end and it barked endlessly.'

'I see,' said Peak. 'Did any of the neighbours complain?'

'Of course we all 'had a word' with her at some time or other. But she never did anything about it. I felt sorry for the sisters the most. The stress really got to Cara in particular. They are such nice girls too. No trouble at all.'

'They fit in the neighbourhood well then?' Peak said, but it was a rhetorical question and so Margaret didn't answer.

Peak learned then about the petition, the complaints to the council and how Janice still refused to accept that there was a problem.

'To be fair we don't understand why she even moved here. Perhaps her previous neighbours had the same grievance. Anyway, it suddenly went quiet and so we thought she had finally seen sense. That was until the dog started to bark again.'

'Do you know anyone who would harm Janice?' Peak asked. Because a barking dog surely wasn't a good enough reason.

'No,' said Margaret. 'I really know nothing about her private life.'

He returned to Janice's house and began to look again at the mess in the kitchen.

'Could she have been beaten with something?' he asked the coroner.

'Not really. Look here. There was a little bit of grease under her foot. And at this angle it was obvious she skidded and fell, hitting her head on the worktop. Here's the trace of blood.' The coroner swabbed the blood, adding the sample on a cotton bud to a long thin tube. He pressed a stopper over the top and added the evidence to his bag. 'My report will definitely be saying this was a freak accident.'

Peak nodded. It seemed so cut and dried and yet he was concerned that he had missed something that might be noticed later on.

Outside Peak admired the street of perfect houses with

perfect gardens. Expensive cars in driveways. The men and women he had seen had looked and acted like respectable professionals. It reminded him of an old horror film he had once seen, *The Stepford Wives*, but was that in itself a bad thing?

'Hello, Inspector.'

Peak turned to see Cara standing at the front door of her house. The perfectly painted door was surrounded by an arch with creeping vines. She had changed her clothes. The formal suit was gone and she was now wearing a pure white summer dress. Her red hair cascaded over her shoulders, while a crown of daisies adorned her head. She looked like a bride.

'You will have a very successful career,' Cara said.

At that moment the sun came out from behind a cloud and hit Peak in the eyes. He squinted. Then looked back at Cara, only to find Angela standing in her place. She seemed to be wearing the same dress as Cara had worn but the flowers in her hair were dandelions, and not daisies.

'A promotion will come your way,' Angela smiled.

Peak rubbed his eyes.

'And you will move successfully into the right neighbourhood,' Elise nodded her buttercup-crowned head.

Peak blinked. The girls were playing some kind of trick on him. He didn't know why but he found it strangely arousing. He stepped away from the victim's door and towards the three sisters' house.

'We're done now,' said the coroner as he led the trolley carrying the corpse out. Janice was already zipped in a body bag.

Peak felt strange. It was as though he were in some kind of crime movie where the crime had already been solved, but the Inspector didn't realise it.

The promotion letter was on his desk when he returned to his office. *Congratulations, Chief Inspector*, it read. He hadn't been expecting it, had thought any further advancement in his career wouldn't happen now, and so his thoughts turned back to the three sisters. They were weird, beautiful, magical – but could they really know the future?

Peak looked at the letter again. He didn't know how this miracle had occurred. It wasn't through hard work. In fact a lot of his recent cases had solved themselves. Like the one with Janice Bailey that day.

His phone rang beside him.

'Darling, our dream house has come on the market!' his wife's voice was brimming with excitement. 'Will you come to see it with me tonight?'

'Yes,' said Peak. 'I've some news too. I've been promoted.'

'This is our lucky day. It's meant to be.'

'Where is the house?' he asked.

'That neighbourhood we always admired. It's full of professionals, decent sophisticated people. There's no chain, it's at a ridiculously low price, and it's ours for the taking if we want it ...'

Peak hung up on Cassie and smiled. Could it be that this was all luck? Or did the sisters truly deliver on their promise when he visited them a few nights ago. The memory of their door opening, Cara waiting for him in a darkened room, all flashed behind his eyes. Somehow he had forgotten being there until now.

*Time to go home.*

He reached for his keys. The smile slipped from Peak's face. A pentagram with a red stone in the centre hung from his key chain.

Then Peak remembered it all: particularly slamming Janice's face down on the corner of the work top; smearing cooking grease onto the tiled floor and the bottom of her shoe; letting the dog in.

He was going to get everything he wanted. But ... what price would he have to pay? He remembered agreeing to something more while he lay with Cara, Angela and Elise, while blood flowed from his finger and was smeared onto a clear stone. He had watched the stone turn red. At that moment he would have done anything they wanted.

Fear and guilt worked into his conscious. What if someone

learned he had tampered with the evidence, made it appear an accident? *No.* He was sure that he had covered everything. Plus the dog, the cause of all the angst, had helped a lot by contaminating the scene.

He smiled again.

The important thing was that Cassie would be happy. More money, a nice neighbourhood and the baby she really wanted to have. She need never know how this all came about.

Peak left the station and climbed into his car. Yes indeed it was their lucky day – even though luck had little to do with it.

'You make your own luck,' Cara had explained. 'And we need your help.'

A brief spark of guilt ignited in his mind, but as he placed his key in the ignition his finger touch the blood stone. The guilt dissipated leaving a sense of entitlement in his place. How long had he worked the goddamn awful job? How long had he been overlooked for promotion? He deserved this and Cassie had always deserved better than he had been able to give her.

He glanced in the rear-view mirror. Cara. Angela. Elise. Their faces floated behind him in a fog.

'We may need you again …' Cara said.

'You may need us …' Angela's voice followed.

'We will always be here …' Elise concluded.

Somehow it was comforting to think that this was true.

Peak turned the key in the ignition and his car fired up first time. The future, for the first time in his life, was looking very bright indeed.

# Survival Of The Fittest

**(Co-written with David J Howe)**

Mandalai Arch turned the speed up on the drill. He was alone on this rock, in the middle of the Equador Galaxy with only two days to go before the new team arrived to take the project to the next phase. Mandalai was a scout. Half British, half Japanese in origin, he scoured the galaxies looking for planets that could be terraformed. This one, almost the size of Earth, had proved to be ideal because it was rich in all the natural minerals that the team needed with which to recreate their perfect 'big bang' - with a little healthy encouragement from intense UV lasers, a chemical 'soup' and a healthy dose of $H^2O$.

The drill bit into a particularly hard lump of rock, causing his machine to judder violently.

'I'm calling it a day,' he murmured into his helmet journal. 'Time to get the real show on the road.'

Mandalai turned off the journal, then retracted the drill until it was safely ensconced in the bottom of the digger. There pinprick sized nanobots cleaned the sharp edges, taking samples of the rock and earth for later examination.

Mandalai looked out across the black horizon then turned the digger around and drove it back towards the huge hull of his ship some twenty miles away from the site. Despite the size of the machine, the strong compulsion engines meant that Mandalai was back at his ship in just a few moments. There he opened the docking bay, stowed the digger and exited via the airlock into the main ship. Once he was depressurised, he removed his suit and placed it inside the cabinet in the airlock. As he closed the door behind him, he heard the familiar click-clack of the nanobots cleaning and sterilising it for its next use.

It was a huge ship for just one man to handle, but Mandalai didn't need any help. He found others were an intrusion on his concentration. He had long ago learnt that the best way to spend his life was alone.

Mandalai walked naked down the corridor rubbing his hand over the rough skin on his stomach. Already the minor changes he had made to the atmosphere were starting to have an effect on his equilibrium. He would have to be gone before the new solar system formed around the planet, particularly before the moon was in place. He experienced a brief and fleeting regret. He missed oceans and the natural tide that flowed within a planet. Even the swimming pool, filled with sea salt, on board his ship, didn't help with the intensity of homesickness that sometimes assailed him.

Mandalai pushed the feeling aside. It was the end of his job here, and he always felt like this. This was the moment when the planet became habitable for humans, but no longer safe for him.

He wandered into the mess, dispensed himself some food from the culinary unit, then sat down at a wide round table to eat alone.

The ship was geared up to take at least eight crewmembers. But Mandalai relied mostly on automated systems that he had built and maintained himself. The craft ran itself, his only involvement was to monitor those systems and chart the course of each new trip, as well as taking the whole thing into the Callistro Dock once a year for an overhaul.

'Mandalai Arch do you read?' came a voice and it was so unusual to hear anything coming through his speakers that wasn't scheduled, that he paused eating and turned to stare at the communications monitor.

He placed down his fork, went to the monitor and switched 'on'.

'Arch here,' he replied. 'Who is this?'

'This is Captain Tara Matthews of the terraform ship, *Arcades*. We are about to dock. We expected you to be ready for us ...'

'I wasn't expecting you for another day,' Mandalai said. 'Can you come back later?'

'No we bloody well can't,' came the voice. 'We're docking

now.'

Mandalai grimaced. 'Give me a few moments. Docking bay will open shortly.'

Mandalai turned off his monitor and cursed. They weren't supposed to be here yet. He wasn't ready! It meant he would have to tolerate them all for a day longer than he had hoped.

He hurried to the medicine cabinet and swallowed the first of the pills that would keep him sane while the terraform crew invaded his space. Then he pulled on a regulation overall and made his way down to the docking bay.

*Arcades* slid into place and anchored beside the large digger as Mandalai watched from the control booth. Once they were in position, he closed the bay doors, and sent an enclosed, airtight platform and corridor carefully towards the door. The platform landed perfectly. The corridor locked in and through his monitor Mandalai saw the door of the ship begin to open.

Four crew members passed through the door. The platform would stay put until the crew of *Arcades* had set up their chemical charges on the planet surface. Once that was done they would disengage and Mandalai would take his ship clear of the planet surface, and leave the humans, and the planet behind.

Mandalai waited by the airlock door as the crew exited.

'Is this all of you?' he asked.

'Yes. I'm Captain Matthews,' Tara said.

'I know.'

'This is ArchaeoTech Skete Barren, and CompTech Dean Robinson. The runt at the end is ChemTech Jude Peterson. I trust everything is ready for us to proceed?'

'You shouldn't have come. You should go now.'

Tara glanced at her crew. 'What? Why? Is everything OK?'

'Not really,' mumbled Mandalai. 'It's not safe here.'

'Oh we've done this several times before,' said Tara. 'I'm sure we can cope with another.'

Mandalai shook his head. 'As I said, you are a day early. The final analysis is still in process,' he said. 'But all indications have been positive. You should be ready to start the process tomorrow.'

'Thank you,' Tara said. 'Where do you want us to bunk tonight?'

Mandalai showed the four to cabins on the second floor of the ship, as far away from his own sleeping space as he could make it. Then he gave them directions to the mess, and left them to hurry away to his own private rooms.

In the bathroom, he swallowed more pills. His skin itched, and his limbs ached. Being around anyone from home always aggravated the symptoms but fortunately the pills soon took effect. They calmed him enough so that he could lie down on his bed and gaze at the flat screen above his head. It showed him images of the sea. Calming waves, rolling over sand and rock. Mandalai fell asleep to the sound of seagulls.

'Arch! Arch!'

Mandalai woke to find Tara staring down at him.

'What are you doing in my room?'

'There's some kind of alarm going off in the mess. I think your samples came back wrong.'

Mandalai sat up. This close to the woman his skin burned and itched more than usual.

'Will you excuse me?'

'What?' Tara said. 'Oh right. You need to get dressed.'

She turned her back and Mandalai pushed back the covers. He glanced down at his stomach. The rash was spreading, which wasn't a good sign for him holding out for the entire duration. He may even have to take his leave sooner than he should.

He reached for the overalls, slipped them over his naked body again. Once dressed he passed Tara, pressed the open button on his door and led her back out of the room and down the corridor. Only then did he remember that he hadn't taken more pills.

On the bridge, Mandalai silenced the alarm.

'Give me the results from the last rock samples,' Mandalai instructed the computer.

'Early signs of natural terraforming. Estimate time of big bang is 24 hours.'

'Shit,' said Mandalai.

'What's happening? What does that mean?' Tara asked.

'The planet is reacting to the chemicals we've already introduced. It's not just ready to be terraformed, it's started to do it on its own. We have to get off this rock before it all goes up.'

'That's good news then. Your work here is done.'

'Not good. This means we have no control on the process. It will be unstable, volatile.'

'I'll wake my crew and we'll disengage. Then you'll be free to leave orbit. We'll have to stay and monitor the process.'

'I don't think you understand. There's no time. We'll need every second of those 24 hours to get clear. I'm activating the lift-off sequence now.'

'But ...'

'I can't argue with you about this. We can disengage once we are clear of the orbit. You'll be free to come back and observe once this solar system stabilises.'

Mandalai withdrew the anchors that held his ship stable on the planet, then pressed the ignition. The rocket jets ignited, the hull of the ship shuddered. They lifted off in a slow, controlled curve.

'I'll give you time to wake the crew, get them up here and strapped in. Once we leave orbit it will be bumpy,' Mandalai said.

'So, how did the shit hit the fan?' asked Skete as he fastened his seat belt.

'We're never quite sure how this happens. Perhaps the planet was close already to a natural big bang,' Mandalai explained.

'This has happened before?' Tara said.

'Only once. I nearly got my ass fried. But we'll be okay. All strapped in?'

'Yes,' said Dean.

Jude smiled wanly, she hated this part.

Mandalai fired the rockets at full jet and released complete engine power into the ship. Then they were propelled up and out of the atmosphere at speed.

Tara, Dean, Jude and Skete were thrown back against their seats but Mandalai remained upright long enough to see the ship fixed to the correct trajectory.

The ship's automated systems took control as Mandalai slumped back. His fingers slipped away from the controls, and he fell into oblivion as the impact of the G-force knocked the wind from his lungs.

'We've stabilised,' said Tara. 'You okay?'

She was frowning down at him with concern. Mandalai felt foolish as he came round.

'What happened?' he asked.

'You blacked out, but not before you activated the autopilot,' Tara explained.

'That's never happened to me before,' Mandalai said.

'We did go up at some speed. It can have an impact on oxygen intake,' Skete said.

'What are you? A doctor?'

'Yes,' Tara said. 'He is. He needs to take care of us. I'm surprised you don't have one on here to help you.'

'I'm normally pretty healthy,' Mandalai said.

'Except when the change is threatening …?' Dean said.

Mandalai sat upright in his chair.

'What do you mean?'

'Terraforming has its side effects,' Tara said. 'We all suffer from them.'

'What did you mix with?' Skete asked.

'Lizard,' he didn't explain more, that terraforming had changed him in ways he couldn't explain. 'What about you guys?'

'Dean is bat,' said Tara, 'and I'm a deer.'

'Toad,' said Skeet with a crooked grin. 'I get all the flies.'

Jude looked slightly embarrassed. 'Chicken,' she said. 'And you three, shut it.'

Tara smiled. 'Never said a word.'

'No one's a wolf then?' Mandalai asked.

'Strangely no. Never heard about one of those. I think they remain the stuff of legends,' Skete said.

Tara was smiling. 'I knew it the minute you met us at the airlock. My skin was itching so badly around you. Had to take extra pills.'

Mandalai looked around the bridge, his mental faculties were returning and he leaned forward to check where they were.

'I didn't know there were others like me,' Mandalai said.

'Those who work closely with terraforming chemicals are always affected in some way or other. It's the curse of trying to play God. If you artificially create life, you change it. Shape-shifting has become the most common side-effect,' Skeet explained.

'Shame you can't choose what you turn into though,' said Jude. 'I definitely would have gone for something like a horse. Anything other than chicken.'

'We're almost out of range. I must have been out for a while.' Mandalai said.

He was uncomfortable with the discussion. Yet these four people seemed to find it so easy to talk about their disability. It was something that Mandalai had never discussed. With anyone.

'You were,' said Skete. 'I injected you with oxygen to boost you back to consciousness. You shouldn't be travelling alone son.'

'I'm usually okay. I haven't had a full change in three years,' Mandalai lied.

Tara and Dean exchanged a glance.

'That's not healthy,' Skete said. 'You have to allow it to happen sometimes. Otherwise it will burst on you when you least expect it.'

Mandalai was in pain. He was crouched in the corridor, doubled up. It felt like razor blades were scouring his insides. He clenched his teeth and hugged his stomach. He knew what was causing this, and knew that it would pass. He just had to ride the storm of pain.

There was a noise further down the corridor, and Mandalai cringed. If someone was coming, he had to control this …

His skin itched and crawled over his body, and he gritted his teeth together as the woman Jude appeared at the end of the passage. She made her way down towards him.

'Hi Mandalai,' she said. 'You still suffering from that take-off?'

Mandalai's smile was more like a pained grimace as he stumbled along the corridor away from her.

Jude hated her job. Hated it with a passion. She had volunteered for the deep mission after her family on Earth had decided that she needed something to occupy her and to build character. Yeah, *thanks family. Shoving me onto a deep space terraforming mission was just the thing.* Even if you didn't take the downside of regularly turning into a chicken into account, then the loneliness and sheer boredom of the job was enough to defeat most people.

She made her way along the corridors towards the mess. At least here there was some different food. Most of the craft she travelled on had food machines made by the same corporation on Earth, and the same machines made the same food … after months in space, the selection of twelve main courses and desserts started to tire a little.

As she entered the mess, she heard a clattering noise from one of the service rooms off to one side.

'Hello?'

There was no answer.

Jude shrugged. There was often some shifting of goods on these craft, especially when they had just moved into orbit.

A shadow moved in the room, and there was a strange dragging sound.

Jude moved over to the small side room and peeked in.

At first she couldn't see a thing, but then, in one of the darker shadows, she saw a hunched figure. There was a slurping sound, as though someone was sucking milk through a straw.

Jude backed away. Whatever was in there had set her senses tingling. Her skin was crawling, and the instinct to run was strong.

She backed away across the room, and turned to dash down the connecting corridor. And ran straight into Tara.

'Whoah there ...'

'Captain ... it's ... it's ...' Jude could barely speak.

'What is it Jude?'

Jude pointed back at the side room. 'A thing. In there.'

Tara looked over to the entrance, and then back at Jude. She walked over to the doorway and looked in.

'It's Skeet.'

She hurried into the room, slapping her hand on the lightpanel and flooding the room with light.

Skeet was lying on the floor by a pile of crates. One of them had toppled off and the contents were scattered around him.

Jude poked her head in, took one look, and promptly backed away, her hands up over her mouth. Skeet had been eviscerated. His belly was split open, and his insides were pulled out and around him.

There was blood. And flesh. And guts.

Jude turned and threw up over the wall. She couldn't cope with this sort of horror.

Tara emerged from the room as the cleaner nanobots began to clear up after Jude. Her face was pale and ashen.

'I've never seen anything like this before.'

She took a couple of deep breaths. The corridor smelt like vomit.

'Jude, go and get Dean. Make sure he's alright.'

Jude nodded and raced away, keen to put as much space as she could between herself and the mess that had once been Skeet.

Tara pressed the call button on the wall intercom.

'Mandalai? Where are you Mandalai?'

There was a pause, and then Mandalai's crackly voice came back. 'This is Mandalai?'

'Come down ... come down to the mess please. Immediately.'

'On my way.'

Tara looked back into the room. Skeet's body was ripped and torn as though by some animal. Her skin was itching, and she could feel the tug and pull of the terraforming process on the solar system that they still weren't completely clear of. This was really not good.

'I was in my room,' said Mandalai.

Jude narrowed her eyes. 'I passed you in the corridor,' she said. 'What had you been doing?'

'Just getting a drink,' said Mandalai. 'Everything was fine when I left.'

'That's as maybe,' said Tara. 'But you were the last one in here.'

Mandalai looked around at the scared faces. Tara was still pale, but had recovered her composure. The young girl Jude was terrified out of her wits, while Dean had a worried frown on his face. Mandalai could smell the fear in the atmosphere. It made the hair on the back of his neck stand up.

None of them had any clue what was happening. Mandalai had tried to warn them, but now it was too late.

'You all need to leave. Now,' he said.

Tara frowned. 'Leave? We can't leave? We need to find out what happened to Skeet. Is there any livestock on this ship?'

'Livestock? No. Only us.' Mandalai was subdued. He had managed to crunch down some more pills just before he was called down, and the itching in his skin had eased off a little. But like Tara he could feel the tug and pull of the evolving planet, even though they had long since left it behind. The 'Big Bang' ripples still followed them and they would leave something in the galaxy that was invisible but would affect all life.

Tara looked at each of them in turn. 'We need to get to the bottom of this. One thing is sure: Skeet didn't kill himself.'

The planet slowly bloomed into colour and movement as the terraforming process continued to work on it. Chemicals and radiation combined to turn the lifeless rock and soil into something which could support life. The air was bombarded and chemical reaction brought atmospheric changes. Winds raced over the surface. Acid rains fell and scoured the rock and surface, steam sizzled from liquefying granite and limestone, and a chemical soup of nutrients and minerals gathered in the crevices and hollows.

Around the planet the new solar system was born. A blast of energy spurted from thin air, as a wormhole turned itself inside out. A ball of fire erupted into the blackness, shuddered and fell into a natural orbit around the planet.

Mandalai knew all this, and from his vantage point, many light years away from the slowly forming atmosphere, he watched as the planet was reformed.

Even at this distance his gut ached. His muscles were throbbing with tense need. The pills he had taken seemed not to be working. His nose twitched. Someone was approaching his room.

He turned his head, and it seemed to rotate right around without his body even moving.

His large eyes blinked once. They seemed keener, sharper. Tuned to the slightest movement.

There was a rap on his door.

'Mandalai? You there?'

It was Dean. The man's voice sounded alien and scared.

Mandalai sat still and silent in his room. Not moving a muscle. Somewhere in his mind he had let go. Allowed the flux and change of the new solar system to seep into his own bones and sinew. He glorified in the change.

His door opened, and Dean was there.

'You there, man?'

There was a swift movement, a cry, and in a second Dean was back in the corridor, blood streaming from deep gouges on his face. There was another flurry of movement, and Dean was on the ground. With his concentration broken, Dean's own defence mechanism kicked in, and the transformation started. With a cracking of bone and a reconfiguration of flesh, he was a bat, flapping helplessly on the floor.

The creature that had been Mandalai pounced again, sharp beak dipping in, claws catching and tearing.

Dean didn't stand a chance. In one last desperate attempt to flee, he tried to transform back into human form, but the attack was too fast and vicious.

He ended his life as a half-human travesty, riven with claw marks and scratches, one arm still transformed into a large bat wing, legs crumpled under him.

Mandalai returned to the darkness of his room, he settled back by his monitor and continued watching the planet evolve. His mind turning to block out his actions, focussing on survival, and how he was going to get out of this. He didn't even clear up the mass of fallen owl feathers that had dropped from his arms as he reverted to human form.

'He has to be here somewhere!'

Jude and Tara were in the Control room. Now Dean was not responding to their calls.

'Have you tried the mess?' asked Jude.

'Yes I have. Several times.'

'Well don't take it out on me.'

Tara looked at the young ChemTech and sighed. 'I'm sorry.'

Jude smiled back. 'It's okay. Sometimes, when we get like this, and the planet is too close ... it's like ... the other natures they sort of take over.'

'I know. And just typical that I'm rat and you're chicken. Hardly the best of friends in the animal world.'

Jude scratched at the back of her hand. 'This damn itching.'

'It's the terraforming out there,' said Tara, nodding her head towards the control room viewscreens. 'It's what changes us. Makes us what we are.'

'How much longer do we have to wait?' asked Jude. 'The chemical process takes a few days doesn't it, what would the physical and archaeological configuration take?'

'Not sure,' said Tara. 'That was Skete's area. But the equipment here should tell us.' She scanned the array of panels and lights. 'We need Mandalai to make sense of this. It's his ship after all.'

Tara hit the comms switch. 'Mandalai? Where are you? Come

to the bridge now please.'

'Do you think he'll come?'

'He'd better.'

'I want out of here. The sooner we get back on our ship the ...' Jude's voice cut off as a weird sensation rippled across her skin.

She moved to the entrance to the bridge, a secure hatch-like door which slid open to reveal the corridor beyond. She looked out into the corridor. It seemed to be darker somehow. She narrowed her eyes.

'Captain?'

Tara looked across at her.

'Something's wrong.'

'What do you mean?'

'Well look for yourself ...'

Tara joined Jude at the doorway. One of the lights in the corridor beyond decided at that moment to flicker, sending flashes of light down the passage. As they watched, the two women saw a shape step into the corridor at the other end. It was large, and while it walked on two legs, the women got a scent that this was not a human.

Jude's eyes widened. 'What ... what is that?

There was silence.

They could hear a laboured wheezing sound. Great breaths being taken and expelled. Both women sniffed the air. There was a damp, animal smell. Something earthy and raw. It made both of them stiffen.

Tara looked at her hand which was holding the side of the door. It was transforming, shaping into a tailored hoof, fine hairs threading out of her skin. She could feel the change coming over her, the ebb and flow of the terraforming planet was reaching into her core, and triggering a change. It was impossible! Surely they were too far away now to be affected?

The creature in the corridor stepped forward, the flickering light flashing off its eyes which were watching the women keenly. As it moved so its shape shuddered and twisted, becoming smaller and sleeker. A bushy tail flicked out behind it, and russet and white fur burst out all over its body.

Tara stepped back, but Jude was rooted to the spot. The same change was overcoming her. One leg was thinning and shortening into a stalk-like appendage, splayed toes at the bottom. Feathers were growing around her neck, and her eyes were wide with terror.

*Fox!* her mind screamed, and the instinct to flee overcame her. With a noise that was part human and part gallinaceous, she raced into the corridor, directly towards the creature. In a second it was on her, powerful jaws slicing through her neck and bringing her to the deck. She screamed and cried and her flesh rippled and changed as the beast savaged her body. Feathers flew around as her struggles quietened, and as she died, her head fell back, exposing her shattered throat.

Tara shook her head. She could not believe what she was seeing. Her friend and crewmate slaughtered by a fox in front of her eyes. She looked around her. There were no weapons on the bridge at all. Just flickering viewscreens showing the planet, serene in its turmoil.

She looked at it a moment, and again the strong pull of change wrenched at her mind and body. She focused her thoughts, concentrated on being human. The one thing which might save her.

In the corridor, the horrific sounds of snapping bone had stopped, and the creature was looking at Tara.

It was a fox, but it was shifting again, flesh running like wax into a new configuration. The snout filling out, fur darkening, growing. Eyes becoming blue and sharp. The bushy red tail curved into a long black appendage which fell down between the creature's hind legs.

She could feel her change coming on again. Her bones trembled as her hands began to change, fingers fusing into awkward hooves. But she couldn't afford to change. This thing, this creature, was shifting into the best form to hunt whatever the prey was. It was evolution at an insanely accelerated pace ... and she was the prey.

Human logic took over for a brief second. She reached out, slamming her hand on the door lock between the corridor and the bridge. But, as her hoof touched the control it was already so far into the change that the strength had left it. As her will was subsumed by the instinct to escape, and her body shuddered and transformed into a deer, the air in the room changed. The wolf paced forward. She snorted in terror as hot breath blew over her pelt. And then the creature was upon her.

Mandalai sat in the control room. The viewscreens were showing a vast starfield. The ship had left the transforming solar system behind. As it writhed and roiled in the process of changing into something else, so Mandalai had changed. The radiation and chemicals had changed him. He knew this. And the pills were not enough to prevent his nature from emerging anymore.

Stupid, stupid humans. They wanted to alter whole planets so that they would be suitable for life, but in the process they had changed themselves. Nature always has a way. There will always be predators and prey. It was the way of things.

Mandalai was the ultimate predator. Not lion or bear, not lizard or wasp, but everything and all things. The genetic and transformative mutations had created an ultimate predator. Something which could deal with life in whatever guise it took.

'Computer. Send the following report to the Corporation … I regret to inform you that the ship *Arcades* was lost during the terraforming process. Despite my warning, its Captain, Tara Matthews, took the ship and crew too close to the new sun. There were no survivors.'

'Report sent,' responded the computer.

Mandalai smiled to himself. At least he had his ship back again. And until the next planet, and the next humans to feast on, he was content. He lay back in his chair and closed his eyes. Behind them swirled transformation, energy and the hunt. He preferred to be alone, but sometimes it was fun to let the beasts inside him have their way, and the memory of the deaths would keep him company on the loneliest nights.

# Sabellaed

When he wakes he remembers the smell of her. A rich musky scent. Pheromones that promise heaven. Metallic. Dark. As melodious as her voice.

He remembers when he first saw her. Her face was turned away, but he could make out the aquiline nose, outlined by the veil of black hair that fell down, covering her cheekbones. And then when she turned, eyes meeting his, the colour was overshadowed by the clear jewel at her throat. Was it a diamond? Or merely crystal? It doesn't matter: it is part of her. As life-giving as the breath that heaves in her chest.

He hadn't been on Novo Mars long and found the terra-formed plant life air alien. The people were different too. They had found religion; everywhere he goes he sees images of God. Revivalists they call themselves. It is mythology to him: as ancient as the faith of the Greeks and Romans. Millennia devotion that no one in the present took seriously on Earth. But the Martians did. Oh not the Martians of old either. They worshipped their own Gods. These are nothing more than settlers, though generations have passed since the first of them arrived. They aren't Earthlings any more than they are Martians. They are Novo Martians.

*She* is one of them.

He remembers.

She was sitting on a bench when he noticed her. It was a park not dissimilar to those created on his own world. Trees, though gnarled, twisted as though bearing the pain of their birth from this drier soil. Deformed they were, but still recognisable, and weighted down with fruit.

It was a lemon tree that she hid beneath.

The sun was high in the stark sky, and yet she pulled heavy black clothing around herself as though she was afraid to catch a chill. He noticed the shiver, the fearful glance at the sunshadow that crawled towards her shelter. How she edged back as far as she could into the darkness.

'Can I help you?' he asked.

She glanced up, then quickly back down – *painfully shy,* he assumed. He had found it endearing.

'I need a cab. Quickly,' she said.

'Are you sick? Perhaps I could take you to …'

'No. Not sick. I just need to find … shelter.'

'I'll get you a cab …' he said.

On his return her perfume was all that remained. He waited in the shadow under the tree for an hour or more. She didn't come back.

At his hotel he walked into the lift; smelt that musky aroma, and then *saw* her. The doors closed before he could react. At the next floor, he left the lift, ran back down the stairs into the lobby. Tortured by the thought of missing her again – though he didn't know why. She is no one, a fleeting connection. But it was enough to begin a lifelong obsession.

The lobby was empty.

Outside the sun burnt at its hottest. Somehow he knew she was not outside.

Later, as darkness fell and the sun dropped below Novo Mars' horizon, he rolled in bed. Fever tortured. Heart burning.

He remembered her. Vivid. Vibrant. Vivacious. But how could he? It was once. A chance meeting under a lemon tree and then she was gone.

He remembered days blurring into weeks. His credit was running out. He needed to find the work he came here for, and yet he couldn't leave the hotel. The sun was always too bright, the days too hot, and all he could think about was finding *her* again. Seeing her one more time.

The nights were somehow less torturous. Sometimes he sat on the balcony, breathing the thin air. He had lost weight since that day, but didn't notice that his clothing was hanging loose, nor that his belt was tightened to the smallest notch.

Food came to his room sometimes. Rare steaks and a tonic

vitamin supplement. A tangy liquid the colour of blood.

Sometimes he ate. Sometimes he didn't.

After a while the dreams became less frequent.

In them he felt her hair draping over his bare chest, her lips pressed to his throat. Her sex clasped around him.

After such dreams, his skin became tender and bruised, as though the wish he made had come true after all and she had been there for real: not just a delusion.

'I'm losing my mind,' he said. The thought amused him as he was speaking to no-one. That was when he realised it was true.

*It's Novo Mars. The air. The people. The religion.* It was draining him of life.

'You need to eat more,' he remembered her telling him.

He was dreaming of course. Why else would this beauty be lying naked in *his* bed?

Dutifully he sat up and allowed himself to be spoon-fed. He took a mouthful of steak, chewed, swallowed. She offered the red drink. These days it tasted better, less metallic, more nourishing. Perhaps he needed it after all?

'Sleep Luke,' she said. 'You'll need your strength. I won't come back. Any more and I will kill you.'

He wakes alone in a stark white room. He is wired to a machine which beeps.

The door to the room opens.

'Hello Luke,' says the nurse. She has dark hair. Blue eyes. She isn't *her*.

'Where am I?' he says.

'You've been sick. Mars fever. It's rare these days, but you had a bad case of it.'

'Mars fever? No. There was a woman. Dark hair, eyes like night …'

'Better sleep. You'll feel better in a few days.'

He closes his eyes, but he hears the nurse as she talks, adding notes to his file: a flat screen on the wall above his bed fills with detail. Nobody types or writes anymore, they just talk.

'The patient has acute anaemia and the same delusion as previous sufferers of the disease. His mind has focused on a dark haired woman. The *Siren of Novo Mars* strikes again. Treatment: intensive dietary supplements and possible synth transfusion. Treat patient as a drug addict. He will crave the attention of his imagined vampire.'

'I'm well doctor,' Luke says. 'No more dreams. No more fever madness.'

'You understand that these delusions were all brought on by the fever?' the doctor says. He is typical in appearance. Fat. Fifties. Fatherly.

'Yes,' says Luke. 'I know that this wasn't real. This … woman … never existed.'

'You'll need to keep taking your medication for six months. Otherwise the virus can come back. You might not be so lucky next time. If that maid hadn't found you …'

'I know. I will take my medication,' Luke lies.

He has been in the hospital for more than a month and is now desperate to leave. He will say anything. The doctor knows this but cannot justify keeping him any longer, he can only hope that the Siren's hold has been broken.

Luke packs his bag, signs the release form, and the doctor wonders if he will survive on Novo Mars. Few like him do.

From behind the reception desk the dark haired nurse watches him leave. She doesn't say goodbye.

'That's pretty,' says the nurse next to her. 'Your necklace. Is it a ruby?'

A different hotel. A new room. He remembers her scent: pheromones that promise heaven. Metallic. Dark.

He takes his pills. Sleeps. Tries to forget. But the Siren never leaves his thoughts. She will be with him always. Sometimes he still dreams that she visits him but the dreams are few and far between. He wonders where she is. Who her new lover might be.

When he goes out, those rare journeys between work and home, he looks for her. There are lemon trees near the hotel … Gnarled.

He will search until his mind is lost.

**Author's Note**

This short story was written, with kind permission from the estate of the late, great Tanith Lee, for an anthology called NIGHT'S NIECES. The story is set in the universe of Tanith's spectacular SF/Fantasy novel SABELLA: OR THE BLOOD STONE and is a favourite of mine. I was very privilege to know Tanith and she was a mentor to me and many other female writers, who she shared her time and knowledge with generously. She is now, and forever will, be very sadly missed.

# Cecile

*1921*

'Male Caucasian. Late thirties,' said Inspector Graves as he dropped the sheet back over the body. 'Someone had a go at him with a rather large knife.'

Death had been in this room for several days now, and the smell of decay permeated the walls, the blood-stained mattress, and the tarnished carpet. Cecile Tovey remained by the door, one hand clamped to the front of her cardigan the other held over her mouth and nose.

'Who was he?' asked Graves.

'My lodger. His name is, was, Brian Ashley. I hadn't seen him for several days though: he'd told me he would be out of town. Hence why I didn't miss him at all.'

Graves scrutinised Cecile. She was young to be the typical landlady, but modestly attired in a dress and cardigan his grandmother would be proud of. Hair tied up, small round spectacles on the bridge of her nose. Not your average young woman at all – *but then,* he thought, *they can't all be flappers.*

'Where did he say he was going?'

Cecile shrugged, 'I didn't ask. Not my job to pry.'

The body was photographed and removed, the room cordoned off.

Cecile went back to her kitchen and put the kettle on the stove. It had been a very trying day and she was certain she would never get the blood out of the carpet. In fact the mattress was ruined, no point in even thinking about hosing that down. The blood had soaked right through and had dripped down over the springs underneath. It was all such a mess. The room would clearly have to be redecorated and refurnished.

She sighed when she thought of the work ahead of her.

Six months ago, Ashley arrived, sales bag and suitcase in hand. He was a travelling salesman, not the sort of man Cecile usually let rooms to, but business was slow and Ashley was very charming.

'Your establishment came highly recommended,' he told her and Cecile recognised the trace of a Southern drawl that he tried to hide: it intrigued her.

'We usually look for long-term guests,' Cecile told him.

'I'm planning to be here a couple of months at least if that fits your rules,' he said.

Against her better judgement Cecile rented him the room at the top of the house, farthest away from her downstairs personal accommodation, which was a small flat on the right side of the ground floor.

Lodgers came and went. Some without paying the bill, and so Cecile had insisted that he paid up front for the first month and that she expected advance rent for every month thereafter.

'The bathroom is on the left,' she said, pointing to the only other door on that flight of stairs. It was so close to his room that it was almost like having his own private suite. 'We don't allow tenants to bring back … lady friends …'

'I'm a quiet man,' he said. 'I like my own company.'

Cecile gave him the list of rules and he studied them carefully while she showed him how the tap stuck on the sink and how to turn it when it did.

'This is all fine,' he said. 'You won't get any problems from me, Miss Tovey.'

Cecile gave Ashley a set of keys and left him to settle into the clean, but sparse room.

Cecile avoided familiarity with the lodgers. Some of them would try to draw her into conversation, but true to his word, Ashley was a quiet man. He kept himself to himself. When she saw the other male guests congregating in the common room downstairs,

Cecile noted that Ashley never joined them. He never passed the time of day with them either.

One morning she was in the hallway, cleaning the large art deco mirror that hung on the left to make the narrow passage appear larger. Ashley came down the stairs, doffed his hat and wished her a good day.

Cecile nodded shyly, but found herself watching his back as he passed through the reception porch.

He had a nice smile. Friendly. Open. Honest. Cecile couldn't help feeling curious about him.

After that she frequently found things to clean or do in the hallway. Sometimes that was in the evening, others in the morning. She tried not to make it too obvious. Ashley was always incredibly polite and respectful.

Cecile wondered what would make his polite halo drop. All these sorts had a failing. Not one of them was as nice as they appeared, but maybe Ashley was truly the exception.

As the weeks passed, Ashley became more open and talkative. Sometimes he would pass the time of day for several minutes rather than a few seconds of greeting.

'Are you married Mr Ashley?' she asked him once.

'Still looking for my perfect lady,' he said. 'But I'd love to settle down some time soon. There's only a certain amount of travelling a man can do.'

Ashley was in his late thirties, ordinary looking, but his smart suit, and charismatic smile made him attractive. Cecile knew her own limitations though. She was 31, plain, and already too far back on the shelf to be considered eligible. It surprised her therefore that Ashley even gave her any attention. But the asking of the question and its personal nature seemed to change Ashley and he became – politely – more familiar.

Sometimes he would even talk about some of the things he had seen and done that day. Halfway through the second month Cecile knew almost as much about his job and products as he did.

'It's a little dull really,' he said. 'I just sell household cleaning things, not door to door, of course, but to the stores.'

He even made polite comments about fashion and clothing he

had seen.

'I saw a nice blouse in the shop window down on the High Street,' he said one evening. 'A lovely pale blue. The colour would suit your eyes, Miss Tovey, if you don't mind me saying. I couldn't help but think of you when I glanced into that shop. You should take a look if you have the time.'

Cecile was a little taken aback by the suggestion. She always bought her clothing from the same store her mother had gone to. She had never even considered going to that fancy store, with its high prices. Even so, the next day when she passed by on her way to the grocer's, she saw the blouse in the window, and the skirt that went with it. Ankle length but fitted, a little bit more of a fashionable style than she was used to, but sophisticated nonetheless.

She passed the shop by and went to finish her food shopping but all the way around the stores and the market she was making comparisons to the clothing. Cecile had really liked the outfit, probably because someone had expressed a view that it would suit her, but she had never been extravagant. Even so, she knew she could afford to buy something nice once in a while, why did she work so hard running the guest house if she couldn't sometimes spend a little of that hard earned money on some luxuries.

On the way back she stopped and looked in the window again. Before she knew what she was doing she was inside enquiring about the price. Cecile thought it a little pricey, but not as much so as she had been led to believe about this shop. She tried the skirt and blouse on. It made her look younger, showed off her slender figure, and the assistant made a suggestion about her hair too, about how it might look nicer down sometimes.

Cecile took the blouse and skirt home. That evening she changed into it and waited to hear Ashley's return. She had taken her hair down from its usual tight knot and brushed it out until it shone. Her hair was long and mousey, but it was healthy and held a natural wave when she let it lose.

She heard the front door open and hurried to her door.

'Good evening Mr Ashley,' she said.

Ashley was almost at the stairs when he turned around. He blinked and Cecile could see, despite having removed her spectacles, that he had to look at her twice before he recognised her.

'Why, Miss Tovey! You look wonderful!'

Cecile shrugged, a little embarrassed by her impetuous behaviour. 'I took your advice on the blouse.'

'Yes. And I was right. It does bring out your eyes.'

Cecile blushed but it was more with pleasure than shyness. No one had ever looked at her the way Ashley was right then. She liked the feeling. It made her world have more possibilities than it normal.

'Perhaps you would like to join me for a little supper?' Cecile said.

'I'd really like that,' Ashley said.

He went away to clean up with a promise to be back within the hour. Cecile rushed around her small kitchen, adding extra vegetables to the broth she'd made for herself. The bread she had made the day before was a little stale, but she placed it in the oven to soften and freshen it.

Then Ashley knocked on her door and Cecile welcomed him inside.

Ashley barely noticed the scant furnishings, the threadbare carpet and the fraying cover draped over the old sofa. He sat down politely and accepted her offer of sherry. She only had a cheap bottle of it, one that her mother had kept for special occasions, but Cecile was impressed when he didn't wrinkle his nose on the first sip. She knew he was the sort of man who had tried finer things.

They spent the evening talking about Ashley's job and his travels. Cecile had never even been out of her small town and so she was interested in the places Ashley talked about.

Cecile began to like Ashley. He was not at all the way she had been led to believe salesmen where.

'That was a lovely supper,' he said. 'And now I must say goodnight, as I'm sure you are tired.'

Cecile had been about to object. She was tired, but she was

enjoying the company. Her nights were often so solitary that it made a welcome change.

'Plus, we wouldn't want your other lodgers to start to think something was going on here. I mean your reputation ...'

'I'd never thought of that,' said Cecile. 'How considerate of you, Mr Ashley.'

Cecile found herself smiling as she closed her door. Ashley was very nice indeed.

Of course her mother had warned her against salesmen. 'Those travelling sorts always lie. Most of them have wives back home,' she had said.

'Brian isn't like that though,' Cecile said aloud to dispel the memory of her mother's words even as they tried to linger.

'Your daddy was a no good bum,' Mrs Tovey had frequently told her, and Cecile had believed it with all her heart. 'Took advantage of me, while running around town with a waitress from the diner.'

Her mother's story ran through her head that night as she climbed into bed and turned off the light. She recalled the hatred, but also the words that chilled her most of all.

'I got my revenge though ... the night you were conceived.'

Cecile had never asked what that meant. She recalled how her mother had said inheriting the guest house from her grandmother was a changing point in her life. Then, just a year ago, Mrs Tovey had died, leaving Cecile the same guest house, and alone for the first time in her life. It hadn't been that difficult to take over, by then Cecile was doing everything anyway. Nothing changed at all in that regard. Strangely her mother's bitter voice was the only thing she missed and she would often exchange dialogue with her in her mind. Other than that, she ran the place the same, with two part-time helpers that came in for a few hours once a week to change the beds and clean the rooms. There was also a cook that came in and made breakfast for the guests. That was all that was needed in this business, Cecile only handled the admissions and departures. She of course, always handled the rent money and checked that the staff were doing things the way they should.

Business had been looking up recently too. At that time the rooms were mostly full. Ashley looked to be staying on, and several of the others had become permanent residents too. Cecile only saw the lodgers on a Friday when she collected rent for the next week. Anyone who didn't pay was put out on Saturday and the locks were changed.

As she fell asleep she found herself imagining life with Ashley. If he stayed around permanently that was. Maybe they'd even have a child of their own, something she had always dreamed of.

'You'll regret it if you get involved with a lodger,' her mother's voice reminded her.

'He's not like the others,' Cecile murmured.

But her mother's voice had followed her down into sleep, telling her secrets that she didn't recall hearing before and wasn't sure she wanted to know then.

She had woken the next day, the horrors of something bloody and evil floating in the back of her mind.

What was it she had seen? A body, dead, murdered. The remains carried away in an old ragman's cart: her mother walking bloodsoaked through gaslit streets. Cecile pushed it all away: it was just some horrible nightmare after all. She had never even seen her mother so young or fashionable, she had always worn the same frumpy clothing that Cecile herself now wore.

Ashley was the cause of this fluctuation in her equilibrium of course. Cecile was attracted to him, her mother would have hated that, wouldn't have even given him a room when she noticed his highly polished shoes, and pristine suit.

*This is my guest house and I will let in anyone I want,* Cecile thought in defiance. But still she felt guilty. A new anxiety, a nervous excitement was unsettling her. The next morning she had to force herself to remain inside her room even as Ashley came down to breakfast. Because she didn't make a habit of mingling with the tenants she knew that the cook would have noticed her hovering. She was also concerned that Ashley might be encouraged too much.

*You encouraged him enough last night,* her mother's voice

said.

'I didn't. I offered him supper, nothing more.'

Cecile went out shopping to take her mind off this new infatuation. She was beginning to let her mother's imagined quips get to her and she felt worried that she had made a terrible mistake by being too friendly towards Ashley.

When she arrived home, shopping bags in hand, she found a note under her door.

'Miss Tovey,' it said. 'Please do me the honour of joining me for dinner this evening. Yours sincerely, Brian Ashley.'

Cecile dropped the shopping bags in the kitchen and left the house immediately. She had nothing to wear of the calibre of the new skirt and blouse and he had seen her in those already.

Later, after shopping unsuccessfully for two hours in the usual stores, she returned to the small boutique on the high street and immediately found a long, chiffon evening dress in pale peach. The colour flattered her pale skin and mousey hair and the kindly assistant, gave her a matching ribbon that she had tied around the top of her head. It had a lovely white feather attached, and was the height of fashion.

She returned home, put away the food shopping in the pantry and she dressed carefully.

At 6.30pm Ashley knocked on the door and Cecile opened it to find him there with flowers and a smile that widened when he saw her lovely clothing. Blushing she took the flowers and while he waited at the door, she placed them in water and picked up her purse.

'You look beautiful,' Ashley said. 'Really quite stunning.'

Cecile felt wonderful. Dressed in this feminine outfit she almost felt attractive: a feeling she was unused to.

Ashley had one of those new fangled horseless carriages and they drove with the top down. She was nervous of it at first and because she was afraid she would lose her ribbon she held onto the feather throughout the journey. But when they finally reached the restaurant, an Italian on the far side of town, Cecile was beginning to enjoy the automobile ride.

The restaurant was fancy: Cecile had never eaten this type of food before and she was relieved that she had bought the new outfit. She fitted in perfectly with the other sophisticates. She had never seen women like the ones she saw there. They were wealthy, confident, some smoked cigarettes through long holders. And the bathroom was a chic haven of black and white art deco, with expensive soap and an attendant that held a towel for the ladies to dry their hands on.

Ashley was attentive all the way through the evening, when the meal ended and they returned to the guest house, he was the perfect gentleman. He shyly kissed her hand, and Cecile felt this was the beginning of a burgeoning romance even though she had no idea at all where it would lead, and only a vague idea of what it meant to be in love.

She was haunted by her mother's warnings though. Sleep became an elusive and indifferent friend. But as the weeks turned into months, Cecile fell for Ashley in a way she couldn't have anticipated and the shyness began to leave them both as the kisses turned from hand to mouth and became a passionate part of their evenings together.

Even so there were doubts. Her own father had misled her mother. He had been married secretly while they had an affair. Cecile didn't think Ashley lied, but the idea of checking his room, in the long hours when he was absent during the day, suddenly became as much of an obsession. Even so, she resisted the urge to pry. It wasn't the right thing to do and Ashley deserved his privacy as much as anyone else did.

'Cecile,' said Ashley one evening. 'My job will require me to move on from here soon.'

Cecile felt her heart wrench at these words. He was dallying with her after all! All of their intimacies and her expectations for a relationship and a child and now he was planning to leave. She couldn't keep the hurt from her expression and thc tears from her eyes. When Ashley saw that she was upset he rapidly placed his arms around her.

'I could stay. I want to. I could … help you run this place and give up the salesman life.'

'What do you mean?' said Cecile confused. She knew they

were busy, but she didn't really need the extra help.

'I mean, we could get married,' Ashley said. 'You must know I love you.'

Cecile was overwhelmed with love and excitement. Ashley wanted to marry her. He loved her! She could hardly believe that happiness had finally found its way into her once dreary life.

'Yes!' she said without hesitation. 'I love you too!'

That night the kisses went farther than normal, but Ashley, always the gentleman, pulled away and quietly returned to his own room.

'Let's keep this quiet from the staff for the time being,' Cecile said to Ashley. 'Until we've set a date at least.'

But the date would never be set.

Cecile had been on her way out when the postman arrived with a letter for Ashley. She took it without thinking, stuffing it in her purse to give him later. She was too excited, having tossed and turned all night, wondering about buying a new trousseau, and furniture for her flat that would make it more comfortable for them both to live in.

She had even forgotten that Ashley's rent was a week overdue: it didn't matter now anyway. Soon he would be sharing her life and they could rent out his room to another guest.

When she returned home, she had forgotten the letter completely, but as she pulled her new cosmetics out of the bag, planning to make herself nice for the evening, the letter fell out onto her dresser. She looked at it confused, for the first time noting the feminine penmanship. She raised the envelope to her face and sniffed. It smelt of cheap perfume, and something else that Cecile couldn't place.

She stared at the envelope. How many of these letters had she seen arrive and thought nothing of them. Her mother's voice had been silent for some time, but now it screamed a warning in her head. She boiled a kettle and steamed the envelope open, curiosity overwhelming her natural instinct to trust Ashley.

The letter was full of words of love. Cecile felt a blinding rage building up inside her. Ashley had another woman dangling. Another woman who ran a guest house, just like her. But how had she found him here? A harsh, violent anger mingled with the sexual frustration that Ashley had been cultivating for months.

It would be a few hours before Ashley returned and so she went upstairs to finally take a look around his room.

Opening the door she found the room to be clean and tidy. An unusual thing with male lodgers. She hurried around, opening drawers, looking under the mattress, but even though there were a few items of clothing in the drawers and wardrobe, Cecile found little in the line of personal effects.

In fact the room was so empty it was almost as though Ashley didn't live there at all.

She returned to her own rooms, confused.

She listened at her door until she heard him come in through the main entrance and head up the stairs. He would change and be down soon, expecting the routine to continue. The meals, the fondling, the promises and lies. She didn't want that here. Not in this apartment where her father had betrayed her mother, and not in any way in the same terms. Cecile wouldn't be used that way. Tonight she would go to him.

As she reached his door, Ashley opened it as though expecting to see her.

'Cecile, I was just on my way down to see you.'

Cecile smiled. She too could hide her secrets. She too could lie about her feelings.

'May I come in?' Cecile said.

Ashley seemed surprised, but a knowing smile came to his lips. Yes he had reeled her in finally. All of the teasing and arousal had finally brought her to his room and to his bed. He stepped back and let her enter.

Cecile remembered the whispered stories, the descriptions of what to do, that her mother had told her, even though she didn't recall when and how she had been told.

The memories were pictured images flashing in her mind. She followed her instincts, let Ashley have his momentary satisfaction, felt the life giving juices pouring into her and felt a strange satisfaction that had little to do with her own sexual enjoyment. Their sexual trysts continued every night in his room after that. And every day Cecile took and kept the continuing flow of letters from the other woman.

As the weeks went on, Cecile noted that Ashley's possessions had slowly begun to filter into her own rooms. She encouraged him to leave them in her small apartment, but would never let him make love to her in her own bed, or even spend the night in her room.

'We have to avoid scandal,' she said. 'Even though we are going to be married soon.'

Cecile never prompted Ashley to make those wedding plans though, and he never brought up the subject other than the casual reference he made to their future from time to time.

A final letter arrived a week before Ashley died. This one was desperate. Frantic. Ashley's former lover, now heavily pregnant and shamed, threatened suicide. Cecile sat down and penned a reply to the sender. She told her how Ashley had betrayed them both.

The woman arrived mid-morning on the second day. By then Cecile had made extensive preparations.

'I'm Carol,' said the woman through her tears. The large bulge of her stomach was proof of the evil Ashley had done to her.

'I want to help you,' said Cecile. 'He has done you a terrible wrong. He deserves to suffer ...'

Cecile took her into Ashley's room, gave her a kitchen knife, and left her there to wait for the man who betrayed her.

She said nothing as the Carol came downstairs some hours after Ashley's return. Blood-soaked and crying she let Cecile take the stained knife from her fingers.

Cecile helped her wash off the blood, then she gave Carol a hot drink. The drink was drugged of course. Cecile didn't want to have any trouble taking the thing she still most craved. Carol fell asleep on Cecile's old threadbare sofa.

Cecile rinsed the knife that had killed Ashley fastidiously in the sink, then she turned to look at the sleeping woman. She dried her hands, and the knife, then she walked calmly to the sofa and began to cut away the clothing that covered Carol's stomach.

Within a short time a newborn baby girl was wrapped in one of Cecile's blankets and placed in the cot, ready prepared, in Cecile's bedroom.

'This is a very nice place you have here, Ms Tovey,' said the Inspector as he sipped the cup of tea she had thoughtfully provided.

'Excuse me, I just need to check on my daughter.'

'Single are you?' asked Graves with a knowing look.

'Recently widowed,' Cecile said. 'It's difficult being alone with a child and running a business. It's probably why I didn't hear a thing that night. Me with a new baby, I've been so tired ...'

Graves nodded, 'I'm sure it's very difficult.'

As the Inspector finally left the guest house, Cecile unlocked the cellar door under the stairs and went down into the basement. Carol's body still lay wrapped in the soiled throw, but Cecile now had the luxury of time to dig a shallow grave in the earth of the basement and bury the only remaining evidence that could link her to the death of Ashley. Afterwards she went into her room and took baby Carol from her cot and cuddled her to her breast.

For the first time she was truly happy. She had everything she had ever wanted.

# Ghost In The Steam

Melanie Argyle pulled her wrap around her shoulders. It was a cold night and a draft wafted in from the partially open door. She was waiting in the foyer of the Savoy while the doorman hailed a Hansom cab. The lobby was dimly lit, and the dense green London smog drifted into the space, floating around her. Cold seeped into her bones. Barely thirty, plain and painfully shy, Melanie was not the kind of woman who received much attention from gentlemen of any sort. She and her brother, Roger, had joined some of *his* friends for dinner. Now Roger was in a backroom of the hotel somewhere, no doubt drinking brandy, smoking cigars and playing some boorish card game. He did not, as usual, give his spinster sister a second thought.

'Miss Argyle?' the doorman said. 'I found a cab for you. The driver is known to me and I'm certain he will escort you safely home.'

Melanie blinked. She was overwhelmed for a moment, not something that had ever occurred before, and the doorman - George was his name - often took care of her when Roger inevitably abandoned her. There was nothing to fear, she knew that, yet she couldn't shake this feeling that something was wrong.

She glanced around.

'You've been most kind,' she said but her voice sounded far away. Muffled somehow, as though she were talking at one end of an immense tunnel that had no echo, but swallowed sound.

George held the door wide and Melanie moved slowly into the fog, wrapping her arms around herself as the damp seeped into her skin.

Pain sucked at her joints. A strange sensation, that made her consider that her usually robust health was in jeopardy. It was as if she were older than her years. *A sudden onslaught of extreme age.* She shuddered. That awful feeling, as though someone had walked over her grave ...

She began to descend the few steps down to the road, but her legs felt as though they wouldn't support her. Trepidation of the cruellest kind consumed her. She was convinced that one more step would mean a great fall, and impending doom. But the thoughts were overdramatic and she knew it. Melanie was not the sort to give in to the vapours, but, even so, she instantly felt the need to cry out for help: an impulse she couldn't resist.

'Help me, George!' she called.

The young man rushed down the steps, reaching her seconds before she slumped.

'Careful there, miss!' George said, holding her up. 'Your carriage is here. Oh look! It's one of them new-fangled ones.'

As though in the distance, a loud whinny of horses made Melanie glance up. There was a blur of movement, a loud thump. Shadows in the mist. A human-shape tumbled beneath the wheels of another carriage that hurried past her own, the smog twisting and moving with its passage. A man yelled, a woman screamed. There was a splash of something red in the gloom, and Melanie covered her eyes with her hands.

Tremendous pain in her limbs gave way to a quick unexpected relief. She regained her balance. Glancing apologetically at George she let him lead her closer to the kerb. She felt so much healthier that it was almost as if the pain and weakness had been completely imagined.

The carriage emerged from the vermilion smog, and indeed Melanie recognised it as a horseless one. A big black monstrosity, with a tall pipe protruding from the top. It made a hissing sound while idling at the roadside. Melanie didn't like it at all. Not one little bit. But any objection was lost as the engine coughed loudly and emitted a jet of steam up into the dense atmosphere.

The driver opened the door and helped her into thc back.

Inside, the carriage looked like any other, though it was perhaps more luxurious than the usual.

Her body was aching again and she shivered with cold.

'Hang on there, Miss,' called the driver. 'There has been a terrible accident. Don't look outside whatever you do. It's best you don't see.'

Melanie didn't look, but she was aware of movement outside: a group of men, lifting something up from the road.

'Oh Lord! He's *dead*...' a voice said in a shocked loud whisper that echoed through the mist and smoke.

Melanie heard the distant sound of a woman crying.

The hissing, rattling contraption finally began to move, and Melanie was jostled slightly in the back but after a few moments the cold sensation that had made her feel ill and sore began to ease. Her concentration returned enough for her to take in her surroundings.

So this was one of the new horseless carriages. It was like being inside a train carriage, only all the engine power that was driving this machine was concentrated, smaller than a steam locomotive would have been. There also seemed to be some form of stabilising influence. Melanie did not feel as though she were too shaken by the vehicle, even though it had appeared so uneven and peculiar from the outside. There was, in fact, less rocking than there usually was in a horse drawn Hansom. It was really very comfortable.

The carriage pulled up to the kerb. Melanie glanced out of the window, and through the mist observed that they had reached her townhouse in record time. The door opened and the driver held out his hand. She took it and stepped down with surer steps than earlier. Then she retrieved some money from her reticule.

'That's all right Miss, the gentleman took care of it ... before ... we left,' the driver said.

Melanie nodded. Of course, Roger would have given George money to ensure her safe return home.

'Thank you,' she murmured. Then she hurried up the steps and rang the doorbell. At the top of the stairs she turned to see the carriage pulling away into the darkness. Steam poured into the air above and behind it and joined the murk of the roiling fog as it swallowed the carriage whole.

In the drawing room, Hilary placed a tray down on the table.

'I know what you're going to say,' Melanie said. 'That you

don't understand why I go. He always abandons me.'

Hilary didn't answer. She poured tea into her cup and sat down in the chair opposite. Holding the teacup and saucer in trembling fingers. Hilary had been Melanie and Roger's nanny when they were young, and now, in lieu of their long dead parents, Hilary had filled the parental void and both Roger and Melanie loved her. Now, even though the two were fully grown, she had become so much a part of their lives that it would never have occurred to anyone that her job was over.

'I would never go anywhere, see anyone, if Roger didn't take me to dinner sometimes,' Melanie sighed. 'It's not as though I'm the most exciting company.'

Above the fireplace the gaslight flickered, as though some of the gas were being drawn away.

'Anyway, the evening was pleasant enough. But …' Melanie halted.

She was trying to remember the evening but all recollection evaded her. Something had happened, which she knew she should share with Hilary, but she couldn't shape it in her mind. It was as though a haze was cast over her mind. Then, a vague thought floated to the surface, it was of a carriage, a black unusual conveyance. And something about George …

Melanie shuddered. That cold sensation leaked into her bones again. Queasiness squirmed in her stomach, and that same overwhelming dizziness returned as the memory slipped through her mind like soft sand through fingers. She sank back into the chair.

'I feel rather odd, Nanny.'

Melanie was feverish, tired, confused, but she was aware that Hilary, wrapped in a thick blanket, sat in the armchair beside her; probably dozing. The lamp beside the bed was turned down but not off, and Hilary had tucked Melanie into bed in much the same way that she had when Melanie was a child. Melanie did not recall walking upstairs, nor going to bed, but the fact that her nanny was present somehow reassured her.

She looked around the room. Shadows cast uncanny light on the furniture but she knew each piece well and still recognised them all in the gloom. Her tall bureau by the fireplace; the wardrobe in the far corner; her dressing table by the window - with her creams and unguents and perfume bottles. All familiar shapes - except one.

In the farthest corner of the room, right by the door, was a dark and unfamiliar shadow. Melanie's eyes focused on it. An unmoving contour. Something similar to the coat stand in the hallway, only there was no such coat stand in her room. She blinked and the shape blurred, moved, as though it knew, for a split second, that she had closed her eyes.

'Nanny?' she whispered.

The shape moved clearly this time, a dark smudge, a fast warp of black. Like the shadow cast by a tree in sunshine, it elongated until it reached the fireplace. The glowing embers suddenly extinguished, and the shadow disappeared - presumably up the chimney.

Melanie sat up, a cry on her lips. She glanced at Hilary, but the old woman didn't stir.

The lobby of the Savoy was cold. Melanie pulled her wrap tightly around her shoulders as she waited for George to come back.

'I have a carriage, Miss,' George said. 'It's one of them new-fangled ones. Runs on steam power. Should be fun for you.'

Melanie felt the cold fog creep into her bones, and a feeling of *déjà vu* permeated her champagne-fuelled mind. She had fallen asleep at the table, and, shamed, Roger had ordered her to go home. Dinner had been nice, and so had one of the friends Roger had invited: an interesting young man who worked as a clerk. But she had been so tired, and had suffered such troubled sleep of late, that she didn't think she made much of an impression. Still, everyone would probably remember her falling asleep, and snoring loudly, until Roger nudged her rudely.

'I don't know why he puts up with me. Or why he even invites me to dinner ...' Melanie murmured. 'I'm a total embarrassment.'

'Now, now, Miss,' said George. 'Let me help you down the steps.'

Melanie held onto George's arm and, as they descended towards the carriage, she was overwhelmed once more with familiarity.

It was black, slightly tilted, as though the weight of the extra gadgetry sported on the top and sides of the machine caused it to bow with the burden. Steam hissed from pipes around the vehicle and made clouds in the dirty cold air. It was almost as if this extra influence was compounding the dreary miasma …

'I've seen this one before,' she said.

'*Miss?*'

'This carriage. It took me home a few nights ago.'

'No, Miss. It was your regular driver last time. Never used this one before.'

'But …'

'Evening, Miss,' said the driver as he opened the door.

Melanie tried to object. She didn't like the look of the horseless contrivance, but the engine hissed loudly, and any protest she might have made died in her throat. She allowed herself to be put inside, and the overwhelming familiarity of the experience made her feel drained. Her bones hurt. The vapour that emitted from the top of the carriage was like cold hard pollution, not damp condensation, and it turned the interior of the carriage so chilly that her breath steamed in the air.

As the driver went to close the door, Melanie caught his hand. His skin was hard and frosty.

'You've taken me home before, haven't you?'

The driver pulled his hand free, but said nothing.

The door of the carriage closed. Melanie experienced the calming gentle rock of movement and then they reached the house. It was as though barely any time had passed at all.

As she ascended the steps to her home, the front door opened and she was greeted by Roger. His face was puce. A colour she associated with him when he was unduly cross about something that she couldn't fathom. She realised he was still angry about her falling asleep.

'I can't stand this!' Roger said. 'I've neglected my duties as a brother.'

'Come back inside!' Hilary said behind him.

'I need air …' Roger said. 'This really can't go on like this.'

'Whatever do you mean?' Melanie said. 'What's wrong?'

'This is really too much. The delay. The long waiting.'

'What long waiting? I came home directly from the hotel. George put me in a carriage. One of those steam machines.' She gestured back towards the road, but there was nothing there but swirling green smog.

'Come inside,' said Hilary again. 'You mustn't blame yourself.'

'Roger … I'm sorry. I know I haven't been the easiest sister a man could have. I'll do better. I promise. Next time you bring someone to meet me I'll …'

'I should have given up long ago,' Roger said.

Hilary consoled him. She led him into the drawing room and pressed him down into a chair by the fire.

'You did all that you could …' Hilary said. 'It's almost 2am. We all need our rest. None of this makes the circumstances any better.'

'Two in the morning?' Melanie said. '… I left the hotel at 9pm.'

Roger paced the room. 'Such scandal! How will we ever endure it?'

'I don't understand …' Melanie said. 'I came home. Straight home. How can it be so late …? Roger. I've done nothing wrong. There is no scandal.'

The grandfather clock in the hallway chimed two as if to call her a liar.

'I mean. I had nothing to work with at all. I even inflated the dowry in the hope of attracting … anyone.'

Melanie looked around the room. It was all too much. Total degradation and now neither Hilary nor Roger would listen to her. What was the point in trying to explain? She had done nothing wrong. All she did was climb inside the steam carriage. It brought her home. There was no delay. She hadn't fallen asleep again - she was sure of it! What more could she say than that?

She felt tired, drained.

'I'm going to bed,' she said. Her voice sounded weak to her

own ears and she was sick of constantly capitulating. Sick of always being wrong no matter what she did. 'Clearly anything I say tonight will not please you, Roger.'

The lamp was turned down but not off. Melanie looked cautiously around the room. The shadow wasn't there tonight. But she remembered seeing it before on many occasions in the last few days. Hilary had retired to her own room but had left a cup of hot chocolate on the bedside table beside the lamp. Melanie had promptly forgotten it was there and the drink had cooled, untouched.

Her body felt strange, as though she were not connected to it.

She thought about the steam-powered carriage and its mysterious driver. How cold it had been inside. How her bones and joints had hurt from it. It was as though she had been absorbed into freezing vapour. And the driver's hand had been icy too! She remembered that! It was all so peculiar that she doubted herself, almost as much as Roger did.

Was she losing her mind?

She made a decision: tomorrow she would return to the Savoy, speak to George and get him to explain to Roger which carriage and driver it was. Maybe then her brother would believe her. Maybe then she would believe in herself. Maybe then there would be no question of her sanity.

She drifted off to sleep and a dark world of fear followed her in with a shadow that was blacker than night. A shadow that blocked out the sun, turning everything around it to ice.

'She had been behaving peculiarly,' Roger said. 'Ever since …'

He found himself looking at Hilary for help.

'I should have made certain … The doorman only uses trusted drivers. That night, I don't know what happened, but she …' Roger broke down. Tears of anger, rage and guilt, all of these things he had hidden from Hilary, and from Melanie, over the last few weeks. 'It's all my fault. I'm always encouraging her to come out with me. Hoping she will find a nice young man ... Now what will we do? There will never be a chance of a future for her.'

Hilary put her arm around him, 'You mustn't blame yourself.'

The key turned in the lock and Melanie stirred. The door opened and Roger and Hilary entered. They were followed in by another man. He was wearing a formal black suit and carrying a leather bag. She recognised him as Doctor McDonald.

'I'm not ill,' Melanie said. She sat up in bed, pulling the covers around her in an attempt to show that she would not be examined.

The doctor stared at her but said nothing. Then he cast his eyes around the room, taking in the dishevelled state it was in. Melanie had not left the room for weeks, and Hilary had stopped letting the maid come in. It was all punishment for some indiscretion that she had inadvertently made. She had tried to leave one night, only to find herself brought back to her room. It was like being a prisoner who had committed some crime that no one would elucidate.

'No change then?' McDonald said.

'None,' Roger answered.

'I know it's difficult but it would be far healthier if this room were cleaned up,' the doctor said.

'Yes, Doctor,' said Hilary. 'I'll get the maid in here now.'

'Maybe we should move her to a hospital?' McDonald suggested.

'No,' said Roger. 'I prefer that my sister stays here.'

'Don't send me away, Roger! Please. Whatever I've done, I'll make it up to you.'

'I think it best she remains,' Hilary said glancing at her and Melanie was grateful for this show of support.

Hilary and the doctor left. Roger opened the curtains and light poured into the room. Then he sank down into the chair beside her bed.

'When are you going to start speaking to me again?' Melanie asked.

Roger ignored her. It was his favourite form of torment, and something he had never quite grown out of since they were children. It had always irritated her because it was so childish.

Melanie pushed back the covers and climbed out of the bed. She walked to the window and looked out on the street. Outside the steam-powered carriage idled by the kerb.

'There it is!' she said. 'The carriage. The one that drove me home. You didn't believe me, but its outside now. Perhaps you should speak to the driver? He'll tell you that I came straight home. Just as you instructed.'

Roger didn't stir.

'You can be such a cad, sometimes,' she said. 'You never listen to anything I say.'

'I'm going out for a walk, would you like to come with me, Nanny?' asked Melanie. 'It's a beautiful day.'

Hilary was sitting at the dining table writing out the menus for the week for Cook before she went off to the market.

It was several days after the visit from the doctor and Melanie had recovered some of her equilibrium. She was getting used to being ignored by Roger, and Hilary barely acknowledged her presence these days either. Maybe the old woman was becoming a little doddery? Now all Melanie wanted to do was get out of the house. It had become claustrophobic. She was determined to go outside. It was time, after all, to begin to trust her own judgement and to stop letting her brother bully her. She was tired of always waiting for approval before acting on her own needs. She *needed* to go out today and nothing was going to stop her.

'All right,' said Melanie. 'I'll be on our usual bench. Can I have some breadcrumbs for the birds?'

Melanie left the house and walked slowly down the steps to the street. She crossed the road, took a turning a few yards up, and headed towards the small patch of grass that passed for a public park. Once there, Melanie took a seat on a bench. She realised that she had forgotten to bring the breadcrumbs. At that moment a woman with a small child halted in front of her. The little girl, her hair curled in ringlets, opened a brown paper bag and took out a handful of crumbs, which she scattered all over the grass at Melanie's feet. A few moments later the area was alive with pigeons; she watched them as they pecked up the crumbs.

'Miss?' said a voice behind her. 'I fetched a carriage. It's one of them new-fangled machines.'

Melanie looked around and was surprised to find George standing behind her.

'Thank you, George,' Melanie said. 'But, I don't need a ride home today.'

'Miss, you *have* to go now ...'

She turned around and saw a big black carriage, one that she had seen before, standing by the roadside in shadow. The driver, wearing a thick black cloak, his face shielded by a top hat that was pulled down low over his brow, appeared to be nothing more than a shadow himself. Melanie was cold: the beautiful sunny day had plummeted into a wintry, dark afternoon. She looked up at the sky and felt the first drops of rain as they fell.

'You don't want to get wet, Miss ...' George said.

Melanie looked at the carriage again. The shadow flowed over the vehicle as though it were a part of it. She winced as a loud blast of sound and steam emitted from the funnel on the top. The vapour was dark grey, rapidly darkening to black as it joined with the spectral darkness that gambolled around the driver.

The rain was coming down heavily now. The park had emptied, the mother and daughter, disappearing as rapidly as they had appeared. Melanie grew afraid. She should take shelter in the carriage, but an overwhelming feeling - that *déjà vu* that she had experienced too many times before - made her resist.

'I have to look after you,' George's voice said, but it was the shadow that pulsed and moved, pointing with a tendril of mist towards the doorway of the carriage. 'This is a driver known to me ...'

'*How do you know him*?' Melanie asked, and her voice sounded like it came from far away.

The shadow faulted, wavered, moved in a flurry like a storm of angry bees.

'We must get you to safety ...' George said again. 'I promised

Mr Argyle …'

The fog swirled around her, drawing her forward and on towards the open carriage door. Melanie noted how this dense, cold condensation was also part of the emissions of the carriage and that the panels of the vehicle held a lack of density. It made her frame ache and she shivered until her teeth began to chatter.

She raised her hand before the open doorway, and swiped it hard against the side of the carriage. Her fingers hit something that appeared solid to the eye, but then passed through without resistance.

She pulled back. Her hand stung with frost-bite and she could see gleaming rimes of ice on her fingers. The coldness seeped along her arm, as snake-like vapour whirled around her, tugging, and pulling, even as she resisted.

'I don't want to travel in the carriage again,' Melanie said. 'Please George, you promised to protect me …'

Loud hissing: the funnel blasted out dirty mist. The spectre sighed as though it had released gas from a tumultuous and overburdened gut.

'I must ensure your safe passage …' it said with a long burning hiss: the voice no longer resembled George's, but something other …

'George is dead,' Melanie said.

'I have a carriage for you, Miss …'

'I saw him die. I saw him go under the wheels of a carriage. No, not a carriage. It was a machine on the back of a cart. Being pulled by horses. It had a large funnel, reminded me of a train engine, only much smaller …'

'It's one of them new-fangled machines …' the spectre hissed.

'You ran out to call another carriage for someone else. The driver was going too fast, he didn't see you in time. The machine was heavy. It rolled off the cart …'

'New-fangled …' the shadow was fading as Melanie's memory returned.

'I heard the noise. I looked out. Your coat … your red coat … all that red.' She fell silent and then, an inner strength, that she had recently lost, began to return. 'It killed you. I'm sorry, George. You were always so kind to me …'

Melanie found herself released from the cold black steam. She backed away from the carriage, the shape was warped, uneven, and now she knew why. The new-fangled steam-powered carriage was incomplete. It was damaged. She saw phantom horses in front, pawing at the cobbles, a basic cart beneath.

The steam shrank back into the top funnel pulling the spectre with it.

Like moisture evaporating from a window as the sun comes up, the vehicle faded until it was nothing more than a smudged black spot hanging in the air. And then that too vanished.

Melanie returned to the bench. Overhead the sun was shining, at her feet the birds pecked at crumbs in the grass.

There was something peculiar happening at the house when she finally returned home. A large black carriage was parked outside. Four horse, with tall plumes attached to their heads. A man stood in front, wearing a long tail coat, and a tall top hat.

Melanie looked up to see Roger and Hilary. They were wearing black. Beneath the veil covering her face, Melanie could see tears on Hilary's face. Roger held the older woman up, but his expression was one of profound grief.

Melanie wanted to rush forward to comfort them both, but found herself routed to the spot.

'So sad,' said a voice beside her.

Melanie turned to see her neighbour, Mrs Franks and her son, Albert, standing on the kerb opposite the house.

'Oh no! What happened mother?' asked Albert. Melanie recalled that he had been away, travelling.

'Mr Argyle's sister was in a terrible accident some weeks ago. She and a doorman were hit and he was killed. One of those new-fangled carriages mounted the kerb outside of the Savoy. Been in some sort of coma since. She finally passed this morning. Poor thing.'

'How terrible!' said Albert.

Melanie heard the distant hiss of the steam-powered carriage.

A sense of unreality overwhelmed her as she heard the words and began, for the first time, to truly understand what had happened.

'No. I'm not dead,' she denied in spite of the evidence. 'I'm here. I'm fine.'

'You don't belong here anymore, Miss,' said George behind her. 'I promised Mr Argyle that I'd look after you.'

Melanie shook her head in denial. At that moment six men came out of the house, carefully conveying a mahogany box down the steps towards the waiting hearse.

'Time to go now,' George said.

She found herself inside the plush carriage. It wasn't cold inside. In fact she felt warm and safe. George sat opposite as the driver closed the door. He smiled and was his usual cheerful self. As the carriage pulled away, Melanie let go of all the sadness and fear she had been holding inside her for some time now.

'That's the spirit, Miss,' said George.

# Imogen

Imogen had been blatant that night. She wanted Michael to know how she felt, wanted to share her love, her sex, her emotions, before they bubbled out unchecked for everyone to see. Day after day she was holding it together but the nights were the worst. She wanted him even though she knew it was a sin and no number of Hail Marys was ever going to change that.

Imogen sat in the dark waiting for Michael to return. It was late. He was often home by two, but that night he still hadn't arrived by four. She was worried. She rubbed her eyes, reached for the cold cup of coffee beside her chair and glanced down at the bare flesh that showed through the slit in her night dress. Her hand slid over her thigh and her fingers slipped under the fabric until they stroked the bare skin there. She imagined it was *his* hand, skin slightly roughened from his job as a carpenter, that touched the intimate and soft area between her legs.

At some point in the night she had dozed in the chair. It helped to ease the long hours, and it meant she didn't see the painful bleakness of dawn struggling through the wintery clouds. Sleeping on the job, so they say, was a dangerous game she sometimes played. What would he think if he came home and found her in *his* chair, with so little clothing on? Nothing probably. That was the thing: he wouldn't even notice. All he saw when he looked at her was his little sister. But then, how could she possibly expect him to think of her in any other way?

Imogen stood and stretched, the thin shoulder strap of her nightdress fell and the fabric slipped down, revealing one of her pert small breasts. She looked down at it. If only Michael would come home now. She was so ready to show him how she felt. Her hand slipped over the fabric, briefly cupped her breast and then she pulled up the strap, covering herself.

Headlights illuminated the room as a car pulled into the drive and Imogen's heart jumped in her chest. Her resolve diminished instantly and she ran for the stairs taking them two at a time. At the top she glanced back down before turning and heading straight to her room at the front of the house. She didn't look out as the engine switched off, but instead slipped into her bed and lay there, heart pounding.

She heard the front door open: although as always, Michael was trying to be quiet. A dull scraping noise told her that the chain was now in place. She lay in the bed, her legs apart, hoping he would come in, but knowing he wouldn't. For a while longer she could make out the muted sounds of Michael moving around the house.

*Work clothing in the washing machine,* she thought. *Glass of juice from the fridge.*

Imogen knew her brother's routine so well she barely heard the noises but recognised them anyway. Michael was very fastidious about hygiene. He would be in the bathroom shortly brushing his teeth. *There*! Water ran into the sink. The shower switched on.

*Oh Michael!* She imagined his rough hands running over his own body, washing away the day's grime. She imagined him naked and hard and eager.

The shower switched off. Imogen's hand rested on her pubis as she listened. Then she heard Michael open his bedroom door. It wasn't long before his soft snores filtered through the wall.

She brought herself to a guilty orgasm. Then lay panting softly. Wishing again that she wasn't his sister. It all seemed so unfair.

In the morning she ate breakfast alone, Michael was still in bed. She hated the late shifts he worked. They barely spent any time together at all. Since their mother died, Michael had taken extra hours, worked harder, all in the name of supporting them both.

At lunchtime Imogen heard the shower again and soon Michael came downstairs.

'Hi,' she said.

'Morning.'

Michael looked tired but relaxed. His blond hair was washed and combed back wet from his face. His blue eyes were bright as he smiled at her. His colouring was so different from hers. Imogen brushed back her dark hair and scrutinised Michael with her hazel eyes. Sometimes she daydreamed that they weren't related at all. Their colouring was so different that this wasn't so hard to imagine. They were in fact opposites.

'How was your day, Gen?' he asked.

'A little dull. I missed you.'

Michael nodded his head but said nothing as he sat down at the kitchen table. Imogen put a cup of coffee - white, two sugars, just as he liked it - down on the table before him. Then she sat down opposite him.

'I thought I might go down to the job centre today,' Imogen said. 'It's not fair that you have to work so hard all the time when I'm more than cap-'

'No,' Michael said firmly. 'You need to stay home, Gen. *That* is your job.'

Imogen felt that knot of anxiety she sometimes felt when she wanted to disagree with Michael. He was pretty stubborn. He took after their mother that way. His ego would cause him no end of trouble one day, but it was impossible to argue with him.

Michael placed his hand on hers and looked at her over the table.

'I promised Mum that I'd look after you. And I will. Always.'

Imogen's face lit up as Michael looked into her eyes, but her brother suddenly blushed and pulled back his hand.

The guilt came again. She shouldn't love him this way. She had to be careful. Surely he knew how she felt? She couldn't help reading into his reaction though, always giving herself false hope. *What if the blush means he feels the same*?

Imogen stood up and went to the dishwasher. Her hands were trembling, her heart pounding in her chest. All the thoughts and feelings she carried inside her rumbled around and yelled 'sinner' inside her head. She began to fill the machine with the breakfast dishes and dirty mugs, but her fingers were clumsy and one of the glasses fell from her hand and smashed down on the tiled floor.

'What the fuck ...?'

Michael stood but Imogen was already cleaning up the mess. She knew how he hated chaos. She had to keep the house clean for him. *That* was her job.

'Mind you don't cut your–' Michael said calmly.

'It's fine. I'm fine,' she answered. 'Sorry.'

She made him chicken salad for lunch. He ate it silently while sipping orange juice.

'Must get back to work,' he said pushing back his chair. 'Cupboards don't build themselves.'

Imogen said nothing but she watched him pick up his tool bag. Inside she knew were all the things he needed to work. She remembered watching him build a cupboard recently. It might even have been a wardrobe. He had caressed the wood, smoothed and shaped it: worked with so much love and care that she couldn't help admiring his hands as they moved. Perhaps that was even the moment when she realised she loved him more than she should.

'Will you be late tonight?' she asked as he pulled his jacket from the coat rack by the door.

'No. This job is almost finished. Should be back early. About six.'

'I'll make dinner then,' Imogen said.

After he left, the house felt empty. Imogen cleaned and tidied and emptied the washing machine. She shook out Michael's overalls and examined the stains. Brown smears marred the cloth. Imogen knew it was wood stain but the splatter made her feel uneasy. It never came out fully, and to Michael it probably didn't matter at all. After all next time he wore them more stain would find its way onto his cloth. Imogen wanted them cleaner though and so she put the wash back on and ran the cycle twice more before switching the load over to the drier.

Then she chopped some vegetables and made a beef casserole.

'Gen? Are you home?'

Imogen jerked awake. She had dozed off in the chair in the lounge again and the hours had passed as though she didn't exist. There had been no dream but the sleep had been deep and sound.

'Must have fallen asleep,' she said as Michael entered the room.

His eyes skittered over her and Imogen realised that she was still in her night clothes and her robe was lying open exposing her leg.

'It's six,' he said.

'Oh good. Dinner should be perfect now.'

They went into the kitchen and Michael sat once more at the table as Imogen passed him a bowl and a plate with a crusty roll on. Then she placed a bottle of red wine and two glasses down. They sat together talking about the day, but Imogen could barely make conversation as hers had been so dull. She listened to Michael talk though. He loved his work and his affinity with his craft was evident in his words.

'I might have to go out again tonight,' Michael said. 'There is one last thing that needs to be finished on this job and there seems little point in leaving it undone when it would only take me an hour or so.'

'Oh that's a shame. I thought we would watch something on TV together. Michael I hardly see you. I'm alone so much.'

Michael looked down at his plate and took a sharp breath. He seemed on the verge of saying something but instead he stood up, bumped the table and knocked his glass over. The wine splashed over the table and onto Imogen's robe. She looked down, watched the wine seep into the cloth like a blood stain on her abdomen.

Michael stared at her, then backed away.

'I can't do this Gen. Not again!'

Imogen heard the front door slam and she stared at the spilt wine and the stain and her empty bowl. Nothing made sense. She had upset him, but didn't know how. She removed the robe and placed it in the washer.

At two she heard him return. She waited downstairs as always, saw the headlights, hurried to her room. It was a cycle that repeated night after night. Sometimes she lingered outside of his door while he slept. She knew that entering his room would be bad but she couldn't help toying with the idea. She would pace silently, waiting for him to wake and find her there. She wished again and again that they weren't related. That she was just some girl that lived in the same house as him. Not his sister, but his lover.

It was as though she only lived when he came home. Each day was the same. She cooked, she cleaned, she washed his overalls and then he would return and fall asleep leaving her lonely.

'Something weird happened today,' she said. 'I waved at the neighbour when she was in her garden. She was looking straight at me but completely ignored me. She used to be so friendly. I think I must have upset her somehow?'

'I'll speak to her,' Michael said.

'It was odd wasn't it?'

'Yes.'

'If I have offended her will you apologise? I didn't mean it. But I might have said something without realising.'

'I'm sure it's nothing …'

That night Michael didn't go out. They sat watching the television and he nursed the remote control as he always did. Imogen didn't mind. She felt alive and calm and happy. She always felt more vital when Michael was around.

At bedtime she followed him upstairs. She waited while he

used the bathroom, then stood awkwardly at the top of the stairs as he opened his bedroom door.

'Michael?'

'I'm tired, Imogen.'

'Can I …?'

'Goodnight,' he said closing his door firmly shut.

Imogen jumped awake as she heard the phone ringing beside her. She had fallen asleep in the chair again. Her hand took the receiver and she pressed it against her ear before she realised that Michael had already answered.

'Good morning gorgeous,' said a female voice. 'I missed you last night.'

Imogen was too surprised to speak.

'Stacey …' Michael's voice sounded sleepy and soft.

'So … I was thinking I might come over to your place tonight instead.'

'No. I'll come to you. Things are a bit messy here at the moment.'

Imogen listened as Michael talked about the chaos at home. She looked around the immaculate lounge and wondered what it was that she wasn't doing properly. She placed the receiver down quietly as Michael finished his conversation, and then she sneaked upstairs and back into her room before he discovered that she was awake.

She felt hurt that he hadn't mentioned his new girlfriend and that he had lied to her about where he was all of those evenings. Clearly he wasn't working so late all the time. He was sleeping with his new whore instead.

Imogen felt a terrible rage. Her ears burst with noise as her heart leapt in her chest. *There was someone else*! But then, what did she expect? She couldn't have him. Ever. She had to accept that and move on.

'Michael, why didn't you tell me you had a girlfriend?' she asked as she poured tea from the pot into his cup.

'What?'

'I heard you talking to her. Stacey isn't it?'

Michael flushed with guilt.

'Gen, we've been through this before. I don't like to talk about these things with you.'

'Why?'

'Because … because you don't take it well. But there's nothing to fear. I will look after you. Like I promised.'

'I'm lonely. I'd like a boyfriend.'

'Don't Imogen,' Michael warned. His face was flushed and he appeared on the edge of anger.

'Maybe I'll go out today and find myself someone. Bring him back here and fuck him. How about *that* Michael?'

'Stop it, Imogen. You know I don't like you to talk that way,' Michael was so angry now, he gripped the table. 'I won't hear any more about this. I'm entitled to have some life.'

Imogen was angry too and she was suddenly not afraid to show it.

'I want a life too. I'm entitled to have life and love and sex, just the same as anyone else is.'

Michael jumped up throwing his chair back. 'You want sex do you? You dirty little whore. You want to tempt me again and again. Don't you remember where that led last time?'

He brought his open palm down across her face, hard, and the stinging slap rang through the kitchen and echoed out into the hallway.

Imogen fell against the sink but Michael wouldn't leave it there. She hadn't been chastised enough. He grabbed her hair, pulling her backwards until she fell down at his feet. He pulled open her robe, ripping at the nightdress.

'You fucking slut. Always lying around half dressed, always flaunting yourself. What do you expect me to do?'

Imogen felt his carpenter's hands roughly squeezing her bare breasts. But it wasn't sensual, or nice. Not at all as she had hoped. It hurt and she was scared.

'Do you know how hard it's been for me? Ever since that day? And it's all your fault Imogen. All because you found those papers …'

Imogen couldn't understand what he was saying, she could feel his hands on her, and that was all that mattered. Even though there was no love in his touch at all. Everything that happened had been leading to this moment. She wanted him, was he finally taking care of everything.

She felt the knife penetrate her stomach and when she coughed, a gout of blood gushed from her mouth. But Michael didn't stop. He plunged the knife into her over and over again, like a parody of the sex act that could never happen between them.

'It's a sin. You dirty fucking tramp. Even if mother did adopt you. So what if we aren't really brother and sister? We were brought up that way and I can't want you. You're better off dead.'

Blood poured on the floor. Something she would have to clean up when Michael had finished murdering her.

She lay still while he enjoyed himself: twisting and turning the knife while the red stuff spread over them both. His overalls were covered in stains by the time he discarded them, pushing them straight into the washing machine. The walls and cupboards were splattered in her blood

'Get up,' he said finally. 'Clean this mess you made.'

Imogen grimaced and pushed her intestines back inside her stomach. The hole closed. She staggered to her feet, sore and barely able to stand but still she hobbled over to the cupboard to find the mop and bucket. Then she cleaned up the blood while Michael sat at the table with a fresh pot of tea.

'I'm going out,' he said.

'Will you be late?' she asked.

'Yes. Don't wait up for me.'

Imogen slipped into oblivion again for a few hours. When she woke she found herself sitting once more in the chair. Her eyes were stinging. She sat in the dark waiting for Michael to return. It was late and she couldn't remember how she got there.

Her robe lay over the back of the chair and she was wearing her favourite nightdress. It was made of a pure white satin. She glanced down at her bare thigh and then back at the window. She was waiting for Michael. She was always waiting for Michael.

A car turned into the street and for a moment the headlights lit up the room. Imogen ran upstairs and went into her room. She lay down pulling the sheet over her.

Michael woke. He pushed aside the covers and sat up. The room was in darkness, but he could see the light peeking around the corners of the curtain. He smelt frying bacon, heard the kettle boil and he knew his sister would be making breakfast.

He shook away the horrible dream that still lurked in the back of his head. Imogen. A knife. Blood. It was all too awful to even consider.

He showered, washed his hair, and combed it back and away from his face. Then he shaved away the bristle. When he came out of the bathroom, he glanced at Imogen's room. The door was closed and he didn't like to go in, but she had left her robe over the edge of the bath.

He quietly entered her room and placed the robe on the chair at the bottom of the coffin. Then glanced through the glass panel to see the rotting face of his sister looking impassionately back at him. His hand stroked the smooth lid of the coffin. It had been his finest work and no one but him would ever see it.

Downstairs Imogen placed a cup of coffee before him. Then a plate containing eggs and bacon, with toast that was slightly burnt.

She was wearing her favourite nightdress just to taunt him, but Michael chose to ignore it. Today he would be kind. Today he would pretend nothing was wrong. He hated to argue with her. Today things would end differently.

Michael sat and began to eat his breakfast.

Imogen sat opposite. The strap of her night gown had fallen off one shoulder and she was wearing red lipstick. He could see her pale pink nipples showing through the sheer satin fabric.

'I thought I might look for work,' she said. 'It's not fair that you have to work so hard to support us.'

'No,' he said a little too sharply. 'I promised Mum I'd look after you.'

'Michael I found something today. Haven't you ever wondered why we look so different?'

'Don't, Gen. Let's not do this ...' he pleaded. His stomach heaved against the bacon.

'We're not related. I was adopted,' Imogen said.

Michael turned away as she slipped the night dress down revealing her breasts.

'I'm not your sister.'

'Stop it. I don't want to do this.'

The satin fabric fell to the ground. Imogen was naked underneath and he could see the pink nipples that haunted his dreams and the fine black down between her legs.

'What are you?' he cried dropping his face into his hands. 'Damn you. Can't you leave me alone?'

'I love you Michael. I want to be your wife.'

Michael felt Imogen's hand stroke his hair. He wanted to die but didn't feel brave enough to take his life.

'I'm sorry. I'm sorry. I didn't mean to hurt you.'

'Death do us part,' she said.

'You're dead ... Can't you leave me in peace?'

'I want to be yours, Michael. Can't you see that?' Imogen smiled. 'This time I'm giving you permission.'

Michael pushed away from the table and backed up to the door but Imogen came forward holding out the knife.

'Kill me, Michael. Make me yours.'

Michael took the knife. Maybe this time she would stay dead. He slashed and stabbed, twisted and turned. Blood covered the floor, the cupboards, the walls. Imogen was still. Then she turned her head and met his gaze with that cold, dead smile pasted on her painted lips.

'I had better clean up this mess,' she said.

Michael stood. Removed his overalls and placed them in the washer.

Then he cried.

# PEELING THE LAYERS

'We saw her this morning,' Meeks said.

'Where?' Edwin asked.

'In the lake, Sir. Floating.'

Edwin stared out of the window, down across the vast gardens. He didn't own Heaton Hall or the estate beyond but was responsible for another inherited legacy nonetheless.

The house was opened up occasionally by the 'Friends of Heaton Hall'. This was one such day, and Edwin always made sure he was there on open days. 'You know what to do,' he said to Meeks.

Meeks nodded and went away to take care of the task.

'There hasn't been a body for a while,' a voice said behind him.

Edwin turned to see Elise standing in the doorway. She was wearing a long flowing dress in the Empire Line style. 'Not getting into the part today then?' he said.

'Not unless you think it will help ...'

Edwin turned back to the window. The sun was rising, dawn was almost upon them, soon the staff would arrive to unshutter the house in preparation for open day.

Elise came to his side and looked out at the flowing landscape.

'Almost show time.' She was amused. She always enjoyed the drama.

Edwin saw no humour in what would happen in the next few hours.

'I've always loved this place,' said Alex as they walked up the huge staircase. 'I really wanted to show you it. It's part of my childhood. Part of my life here in Manchester. Long before we met.'

'I know,' said Victor. 'And I want to know everything about you ...'

'It's odd though. They stopped opening the place regularly to visitors. And I haven't been since ... I was about thirteen, I guess.'

'Why does the place mean so much to you?' Victor asked.

'Perhaps I had a romantic view of it. As a child ... Linked to puberty probably. Why else?'

'That's the shrink part of you talking,' Victor said as he smiled at her. Something he rarely did.

Alex didn't respond. She too was given to being serious. Instead she considered why Heaton Hall still intrigued her.

'I like old houses,' she said as though speaking her thoughts aloud.

'This is more a folly though ... Like Penrhyn Castle. Which you also loved as I recall.'

'Not as much as this place.'

They passed through a roped-off bedroom that appeared ready to sleep in. Alex studied all of the old furniture but made no comment. It amused Victor, because no one embraced the modern world more than her. She never liked anything in their house that wasn't in vogue and the style of these old castles and houses she wanted to visit was so far removed from her own personal taste that it was impossible to reconcile her fascination with the old against her obsession with the new. She loved to see these places. Even now her eyes glowed with interest as she paused at the rope and stared into the gloomy room.

Victor found himself wondering what it was she sought in the darkened corners of the space. Did she imagine the original owner's wife lounging on the chaise? Did she romanticise the apparent simplicity of their opulent wealth? He tried not to analyse her but it was difficult not to. Alex was, on the surface, just as calm and collected and professional as Victor, but often he felt that she had layers that one day he may peel away. What was underneath intrigued him the most. There was something about her past, something from her childhood that led her into the psychiatry profession and it wasn't the same thing that motivated his career choice. Victor wanted to learn what that was.

'Do you like history?' he asked her.

'I'm interested in it of course. It's part of what makes us who we are … the baggage our parents brought from the past.'

Alex turned away from the bedroom and moved on deeper into the house. Victor followed. She ensnared him.

'Tell me about the last time you came here …' he said.

'I don't remember the last time exactly. More a culmination of times. There was a summer spent paddling in the children's pool in the kids' play area. I haven't shown you that yet. But there's swings, slide, seesaw … the usual. But also this shallow paddling pool. It was a very hot summer that year. I recall going on the boats on the lake … a few times over the years too. Not many. Lots of walking around the grounds. I always loved looking in the house. I probably did that most. Yet … I didn't remember the rooms. This feels like I'm seeing it all for the first time.'

'What else did you do here?'

'Horse riding. I wasn't very good, but I came here on the occasional Saturday. I was at high school by then. Maybe eleven or twelve. I had a friend who had a horse and once or twice I'd spent a weekend helping her muck out the stable. But as girls are, she and another friend were cruel. They laughed because I had to wash my hands before we ate our lunch. I don't recall if that was why I didn't help again. But I liked the horses. Wanted to ride. So I came here instead.'

'Who brought you to the park on Saturdays?'

'No one.'

'Did you come with friends?'

'No.'

'Totally unsupervised?'

'I was never afraid to be alone.'

Victor knew that this was true. Alex was comfortable in her own company. Perhaps more so than in his.

He took her hand but her fingers slipped from his grasp as she hurried on into another room.

Why was it she was still so elusive? Even after all this time. He followed her. She was a shadow, a ghost, a flame that would never burn out.

'Can I help you?' said a voice beside him.

'I'm here with …' he pointed in the direction Alex had flown.

Then he turned to find a beautiful woman watching him. She wasn't the usual type to work in a heritage site – usually retired volunteers were on hand to give historical context.

'This part of the house is off limits,' the woman said. 'I'll show you back to the Friends' tour guide.'

'But my fiancée …' he said.

'Don't worry. Someone will guide her back.'

Victor followed the woman down a staircase he hadn't previously noticed. It was a back entrance … a servants' staircase perhaps.

'Through that door,' she said, pointing to a large framed, oversized door ahead.

Victor went towards it. As he opened the door he turned to thank the woman, but she had already moved on. Probably through some secret passage-way. He would enjoy telling Alex when she finally found her way back to the group.

'This way …' said the guide.

Victor tagged on at the back. He searched the faces of the others on the tour. Then followed a half an hour of history, and explanations, none of which he could take in. The truth was he was growing more and more concerned that Alex hadn't found her way back.

The tour came to an end and the group was escorted outside of the house. Victor looked around with dismay. 'Where is she?' he muttered to himself.

'You okay there?' said a teenage girl who was walking a small dog.

'My fiancée … I think she's still inside.'

The doors of the house were now firmly closed. Victor tried them. They appeared to be locked. He knocked. But no one came.

'She can't be,' said the girl. 'That place has been shut for ages. They don't let anyone look inside anymore.'

'But I just went on the tour.'

'What tour?'

Victor looked back at the door from which he had just left the house. There was a sign now pasted on it.

HEATON HOUSE. CLOSED FOR RENOVATION.

Victor was confused. He walked towards the car park and searched for his car. There were cars of all kinds there. But not his sparkling new Jaguar. The area looked different too. Unkempt. Dated.

He became aware of the clothing that the people around him wore also. It was wrong somehow. Though not being much for fashion he couldn't be sure why.

He returned to the house. Walking the perimeter, he searched for Alex. Where was she? How had she simply disappeared? He was frantic and then he recalled his mobile phone. He went into his pocket. He'd call her. This had to be some kind of prank.

The phone was warm in his cold hands. The weather had gone from very warm summer to a cold early autumn. He dialled Alex's number, but the phone rejected it.

There was no signal.

He went back to the house. Banged now on the door. No one came to open it. Victor's nerve cracked when he looked around and found the grounds now totally deserted. Unlike Alex he did not like to be alone. Especially in open places.

Victor experienced a feeling of vulnerability. His head hurt. His eyes stung and panic tightened his throat.

Where was the teenager with the dog at least?

Not knowing what to do, Victor reasoned he must find a park employee to help him find Alex. He walked down the long driveway from the house toward the boating lake. But this place was deserted too. The payment booth was closed. No boats were on the lake. Instead they were all stored and tied up on the island in the centre. Victor climbed over the fence and walked toward the edge of the lake. Then he saw her. *Floating.* Like an angel in a calm sea. Beautiful and … dead. Very dead …

'Sir?'

Victor snapped out of his reverie.

'Did you want to hire a boat?'

The area was buzzing with life once more. Victor blinked. He saw the row boats and pedalos working their way around the lake. He found he was squinting into now glaring sunlight. Gone was the autumnal air that had stung him.

'Body …' he said.

'Oh, that old tale …'

'Tale?' said Victor.

'About the woman who was found in the lake. About twenty years ago now. She was thirty-two. With her fiancé. They went into the house but she vanished. Then, later, she was found drowned in the lake.'

'A story …?'

'Well. No one ever really found a body here. But the fiancé insisted he saw her. They dredged the lake but they never found her.'

Victor looked down at his hands. He saw now the markings of liver spots. Markings that hadn't been there before. Confused he headed back up to the house. There he saw a sign saying 'Open Day'.

'Hello,' said a woman standing by the door. 'We have one space left on the final tour if you're alone.'

Victor looked up and recognised her from somewhere. She wasn't the sort he'd expect to find working a heritage site. They were usually retired folks who had lots of historical information to impart.

Victor had a feeling of *déjà vu* as he followed her inside.

They went up a staircase. He didn't speak as he followed. But the more they walked, the more familiar the woman became to him …

'Victor?' she said.

She gave him one of her rare smiles.

'*Alex …*'

She took his hand. 'What did you want to know?'

'Know?'

'There's a reason you wanted to visit something from my

childhood. Are you having second thoughts?'

Victor shook his head. 'Never.'

'Not even …'

He pulled her to him. 'Never Alex. I love you.'

She slipped from his grasp. And though she was a grown woman of thirty-two, she ran on through the house like a schoolgirl being chased by a horny, unwelcome suitor.

Victor rose to the bait and gave chase. He forgot who he was sometimes. That serious side faded. Listening to the crazed minds of those he treated could alter a man. It could taint your soul. But Alex … she *freed* him.

She ran downstairs. One of the old volunteers came out of a room in the house to frown at them. But Alex didn't notice. She was clear of some burden that her childhood had given her. Now she let that inner, frightened creature loose.

He followed. He felt like a dog in heat. He had to possess her. Always. But she was light on her feet, and Victor, not being the sporty type, struggled to keep up.

He caught her - because she wanted to be caught - by the boating lake.

By then the mid-afternoon sun was fading, the park rapidly emptying. Victor kissed Alex in an uncharacteristic display of public affection.

'What's got into you?' she asked.

'You have. The layer we just peeled.'

'What layer?'

'I know Alex. I know what happened to you.'

Alex frowned.

'I know now why you became a shrink. You genuinely feel you can help.'

'Of course. That's why any of us went into the profession isn't it? That and interest in the human psyche.'

'Murderers fascinate me. So do victims …'

'You work with the darkest … I know,' she said.

Victor noted that Alex's frown remained. He could see that vulnerable child now. The one who couldn't remember what the rooms in the house looked like. But so wanted to return to look into the dark shadows for that deep horror she had faced.

The layer he had been hoping to peel fell away as he saw the fear and doubt appear on her face.

'What happened in the house?'

'What do you mean?'

'You ran away … got lost.'

'I could never get lost in there,' she said. 'It's outside that …'

She fell silent.

Victor picked the scab. 'The horse riding …'

'What about it?'

'It's a metaphor for another memory.'

'Don't be ridiculous …'

'What was the name of the horse you rode?'

'I don't recall …'

'You don't recall because it never happened. How many times did you go riding?'

Alex's frown deepened. 'What is this?'

They were by the boat house now. Alex looked away from him, over at the lake. 'Should we hire a boat? I like to row …' she said.

She took his hand, but Victor could still see the frown. His fascination with her grew. Maybe he hadn't peeled the right layer yet. But there was abuse there. He knew it.

Her bravado had gone. For the first time he saw her uncertain and the normal confidence she exuded appeared to be a distant memory. She examined his face with an expression akin to *fear* …

'The lake …' he murmured.

'What?'

'*Floating*. In the lake.'

'Stop it Victor!' …

Victor stared out over the water. There was no body in the lake. But he knew she had been there twenty years ago.

'Sir?' said the boat attendant. 'Did you want to hire a boat?'

Victor turned away and walked back up the hill towards the

house. The door was open and the beautiful girl who had guided him down the back stairs earlier was waiting.

'Is this hell?' he asked her.

'Come inside Victor,' she said. 'I'm Elise.'

He followed her in. They passed the tour unseen as they walked back upstairs.

'I saw her in the lake. I peeled and prodded the wound of her childhood. *I caused it.*'

He noticed that Elise was wearing an Empire Line gown. She took his hand.

'You come back here every year, trying to make sense of Alex's disappearance,' she said, 'but still you don't remember what happened.'

Victor shook his head.

'It's time we peeled *your* layers ...' said Edwin behind them.

Victor turned and looked at the man. He was familiar, but Victor did not know why.

'*Remember* ...' said Elise.

Edwin took Victor's other hand ...

*'Stop it Victor!' said Alex.*

*'Come on Alex, we're getting married next week ...'*

*'Not here. What's the matter with you?'*

*The boathouse was deserted and the park was just a short time from closing. Across the lake the boats were already moored, and the attendants had left, locking the barrier to prevent anyone coming into this area unsupervised. Victor and Alex had hidden for devilment – Alex's idea.*

*'There's no one around. We could go for a swim at least. Maybe cross to the island and borrow a boat for a little while.'*

*'Okay,' Victor said.*

*Alex stripped down to her bra and pants and Victor stripped to his underpants. They left their clothing by the boathouse and then, sitting on the edge of the concrete mooring, they dangled their feet into the water.*

*Alex braved it first. Victor wondered if it was because she felt vulnerable in her underwear. Once submerged, she pushed away from the side and began to swim.*

*Victor slid into the water. It was cold and his breath caught as it engulfed him. Then, following Alex's lead he swam out into the lake. It was bracing and fun. Moving made him less aware of the cold and his limbs naturally warmed up as he followed her. Alex was a good swimmer, better than Victor, but he was secure enough that he knew he could make it all the way across to the island.*

*'We're professionals,' he thought as guilt for any misdemeanour often reared its head in the middle of the fun. 'We shouldn't be here ...'*

*One of the things that Victor loved about Alex was her spontaneity. But it also worried him. She seemed so serious and controlled and then, there were these moments, flashes really, of ... he couldn't even think of the correct word but the closest was rebellion.*

*Alex reached the island and was carefully selecting a boat. She pushed one into the water and then she watched Victor as he swam towards her.*

*Before untying it, Alex placed the two oars in the boat.*

*'Come on Victor you slow poke!' she called.*

*That layer again flashed across her face. Bravery, strength. She wasn't afraid of anything.*

*Victor reached the boat.*

*'Get in,' Alex said. She untied the mooring rope as soon as he was in place. Then she climbed in beside him.*

*Victor was tired from the cold water and the lack of practice in swimming such a distance. He rowed the boat into the centre of the lake though, and there they sat, floating on the water.*

*Then Alex took over the rowing for a while. Victor watched as her arms moved with ease. His future wife was strong mentally and physically.*

*'Tell me more about your childhood ...' he asked again.*

*'Oh, that old chestnut!' she laughed. 'As much as you'd love to be rescuing me from a horrific past, I will have to disappoint you, darling. I didn't have a terrible childhood. In fact, my*

*parents were pretty boring. Dad, as you know, was a paramedic. Mum, a nurse. They both wanted me to become a doctor. But I don't think they expected me to be a psychiatrist.'*

*Victor knew this. She'd told him several times. But what she didn't like to talk about was the day they both died. It was a layer he really wanted to peel ...*

*'Darling,' he said. 'How did they ...?'*

*'You're tired,' she said. 'I'll drop you back near the boathouse.'*

*Victor didn't argue because he really believed he couldn't make the swim back.*

*After he climbed out of the boat, he pulled on his clothes as Alex rowed back to the island. She dragged the boat back into place and firmly tied the mooring rope. Then she waved to him and waded back into the water. He watched her silent grimace as the cold touched her skin. She mimed a shudder for him and then laughed, plunging confidently back into the water.*

*She took up a strong crawl but as she reached the halfway point she paused. Treading water, she began to look around her. Then Victor became aware of a vibration that flowed through the water. The land beneath his feet shook. Surely it couldn't be an earthquake? Not here, in England!*

*He cupped his hands around his mouth and called to her. 'Keep swimming!'*

*Alex began again and then the cold of the water found the tiredness in her limbs. She wasn't as strong as she thought she was.*

*Cramp! Victor thought.*

*'Lie back!' he yelled. 'Float, Alex!'*

*She tried to.*

*Victor was rooted to the spot with fear. He'd never faced any real adversity and now, not being the best swimmer, he was torn between self-preservation and the fear that she would drown.*

*'I'll get help!' he cried.*

*Alex turned, she fought against the cramp and struggled closer to the boat house. But the pain swallowed her, as did the water.*

*'Alex!' he yelled. 'Oh God! Alex!'*

*'What are you doing here?' said a voice behind him.*

*Victor turned to see the boat attendant.*

*'There's a woman. Drowning in the lake!'*

*The attendant looked out. 'I don't see anyone.'*

*'She went under! Please you have to help her!'*

*The attendant went and unlocked the boathouse. Inside, a petrol-powered boat was moored in a shallow gulley of water. He climbed in and drove the boat out.*

*'Over there!' shouted Victor. 'She was over there!'*

*The man steered the boat to the spot. He even jumped into the water and swam under.*

*But there was no sign of Alex …*

'It was my fault,' said Victor to Elise.

Edwin and Elise released his hands.

'No,' said Edwin. 'It was unfortunate. She was in the wrong place at the wrong time.'

'If I hadn't pushed her to talk … If I had been brave enough to go back in the water for her …'

Edwin and Elise exchanged a look. *Tell him,* Elise thought. Edwin nodded. It was time.

'Alex is caught in a rift,' Edwin said. 'A time-shift. And you are linked to her. It's why you come back every year and relive this same moment over and over. It's also why you'll leave here today and not remember coming back.'

'I don't understand,' said Victor. 'I lost the love of my life. She drowned.'

'She's not dead,' said Elise. 'Take comfort, Victor. She'll never be dead.'

'This is old land,' said Edwin. 'It belongs to creatures who choose never to be seen. But sometimes their world leaks out into ours. Alex is caught there. Eventually they will pull her across into their world permanently. Time moves differently in the underworld.'

'Who are you people?' asked Victor.

'Guardians,' said Edwin. 'We're here to make sure this never happens again.'

Elise escorted Victor out of the house, and back to his own time. Then she returned to the upstairs room that overlooked the gardens.

'He'll be all right,' Edwin said.

'I know. But how many more years must he suffer?'

'You know what they are like. They'll take her in eventually. It just takes time. For *empathy* to set in.'

'Do they even understand emotions as we do?' Elise asked. 'After all the fae aren't human and never will be.'

'Unlike us, who once were ...' Edwin said.

Elise stood beside him and gazed out over the gardens as though she were remembering a time when she too was caught between worlds.

It's time,' said Elise.

A light brighter than human eyes could tolerate burned in the corner of the room. Elise and Edwin turned and walked towards it. Elise suspected they'd be back. Not too soon, but certainly in a year's time when the *flow* happened and the other dimension leaked into the world of humans. Then, Edwin and Elise would have to return. So may Alex and Victor, to live their day over again.

'I hope they free her soon,' Elise said.

'So do I. The pain of being caught ... like that ...'

'Don't think of it,' Elise said. 'We've done the best we can.'

They melded with the light and then Meeks, following behind, watched as the two unnatural beings became part of an old and faded painting. As the couple turned to face outward, he threw a white cloth over the frame plunging the picture into darkness.

The portal had closed.

Meeks looked around the room confused. He couldn't recall what he had done all day. He picked up his broom and began to sweep away the dusty footprints left by the visitors.

# COPYRIGHTS

LEGENDS OF CTHULHU

*The Bastet Society* © 2018 Sam Stone. First published in *Tails of Terror,* Golden Goblin Press, December 2018.
*The Cuban Curse* © 2019 Sam Stone. Original to this collection.
*Breaking Point* © 2017 Sam Stone. First published in *Return Of The Old Ones,* Dark Regions Press, January 2017.
*Amatu* © 2019 Sam Stone. Original to this collection.
*Keeping The Faith* © 2019 Sam Stone. First published in *The Summer Of Lovecraft,* Dark Regions Press, July 2019.
*Sacrifice* © 2017 Sam Stone. First published in *Through A Mythos Darkly*, PS Publishing, October 2017.

OTHER NIGHTMARES

*Walking the Dead* © 2012 Sam Stone. First published as an original audio story with *Zombies In New York And Other Bloody Jottings,* AudioGo, October 2012.
*The Last Resort* © 2013 Sam Stone. First published in *Fear The Reaper,* Crystal Lake Publishing, October 2013.
*Three Sisters* © 2016 Sam Stone. First published in *The Black Room Manuscripts,* Sinister Horror Company, July 2016.
*Survival Of The Fittest* © 2015 Sam Stone and David J Howe. First published in *Flesh Like Smoke,* April Moon Books, July 2015.
*Sabellaed* © 2015 Sam Stone. First published in *Night's Nieces,* Immanion Press, December 2015.
*Cecile* © 2015 Sam Stone. First published in *Tales Of The Female Perspective,* Chin Beard Press, May 2015.
*Ghost In The Steam* © 2019 Sam Stone. Original to this collection.
*Imogen* © 2012 Sam Stone. First published in *Siblings,* Hersham Horror, August 2012.
*Peeling the Layers* © 2019 Sam Stone. First published in *Terror Tales of Northwest England,* Telos Publishing, September 2019.

# About the Author

SAMANTHA LEE HOWE began her professional writing career in 2007 and has been working as a freelance writer for small, medium and large publishers, predominately writing horror and fantasy under the pen name SAM STONE. This body of work includes 13 novels 5 novellas, 3 collections, over 40 short stories, an audio drama and a *Doctor Who* spin-off drama, *The White Witch Of Devil's End*, that went to DVD.

Samantha has now turned her hand to thriller writing with her first novel in this genre due out in 2020.

A former high school English and Drama teacher, Samantha has a BA (Hons) in English and Writing for Performance, an MA in Creative Writing and a PGCE in English.

Before teaching she had many careers from running her own drama, dance and singing school to mobile hairdressing. All of which she feels give her a wealth of experience in various roles and good communication skills.

Samantha lives in Lincolnshire with her husband, *Doctor Who* historian and writer, David J Howe, and their two cats Leeloo and Skye. She is the proud mother of a lovely daughter called Linzi.

Her works can be found in paperback, hardback, ebook, screen and audio.

More information on Samantha's work can be found at www.samanthaleehowe.co.uk

# Other Titles by Sam Stone

*THE VAMPIRE GENE SERIES*
Horror, thriller, time-travel series.
1: KILLING KISS
2: FUTILE FLAME
3: DEMON DANCE
4: HATEFUL HEART
5: SILENT SAND
6: JADED JEWEL

*JINX CHRONICLES*
Hi-tech science fiction fantasy series
1: JINX TOWN
2: JINX MAGIC
3: JINX BOUND

*KAT LIGHTFOOT MYSTERIES*
Steampunk, horror, adventure series
1: ZOMBIES AT TIFFANY'S
2: KAT ON A HOT TIN AIRSHIP
3: WHAT'S DEAD PUSSYKAT
4: KAT OF GREEN TENTACLES
5: KAT AND THE PENDULUM
6: TEN LITTLE DEMONS
THE COMPLETE LIGHTFOOT

THE DARKNESS WITHIN
Science Fiction Horror Short Novel

CTHULHU AND OTHER MONSTERS
ZOMBIES IN NEW YORK AND OTHER BLOODY JOTTINGS
Short story collections

POSING FOR PICASSO
Supernatural Thriller

# Other Telos Horror Titles

DAVID J HOWE
TALESPINNING

FREDA WARRINGTON
NIGHTS OF BLOOD WINE

PAUL LEWIS
SMALL GHOSTS

DAWN G HARRIS
DIVINER

STEVE LOCKLEY & PAUL LEWIS
KING OF ALL THE DEAD

SIMON MORDEN
ANOTHER WAR

GRAHAM MASTERTON
THE HELL CANDIDATE
THE DJINN
RULES OF DUEL (WITH WILLIAM S BURROUGHS)
THE WELLS OF HELL

RAVEN DANE
ABSINTHE AND ARSENIC
DEATH'S DARK WINGS

*CYRUS DARIAN STEAMPUNK SERIES*
CYRUS DARIAN AND THE TECHNOMICRON
CYRUS DARIAN AND THE GHASTLY HORDE
CYRUS DARIAN AND THE WICKED WRAITH